AF207522

LOVE, LIES, AND LOYALTY

a Rico's Girls novel

by
Shelia Sewell

If you purchased this book without a cover you should be aware that this book is stolen property. It was reported as "unsold and destroyed" to the publisher, and neither the author nor the publisher has received any payment for this "stripped book."

ISBN-13: 978-0-692-96661-7

Love, Lies, and Loyalty

Copyright © 2017 by Shelia Sewell

All rights reserved. This book or parts thereof may not be reproduced in any form, stored in any retrieval system, or transmitted in any form by any means—electronic, mechanical, photocopy, recording, or otherwise—without prior written permission of the publisher, except as provided by United States of America copyright law.

This is a work of fiction. Names, characters, places, and incidents either are the products of the author's imagination or are used fictitiously. Any resemblance to actual persons, living or dead, businesses, companies, events, or locales is entirely coincidental.

For permission requests, please contact the author via the "Contact" page on the following website: www.authorsheliasewell.com.

Dedication

First, this book is dedicated to all of the women who played a part in raising me: my mother, Jessie, who instilled in me at an early age the importance of reading and education, working hard, and always being there for others especially family. My grandmother, whom I still call Mama, because I lived with her while my mom attended college. She taught me humility and how to take care of a home. She also made the best tea cakes and lemon meringue pie! My aunts Willistine, Merlin, and my heavenly aunts Jackie and Lillie for being like my big sisters. Thank you for helping me with homework, combing my hair, sneaking me into clubs (Lillie), and sharing a little bit of yourselves with me.

Second, I dedicate this book to those who I have mothered. To my beautiful first born, DeAna. Thank you for allowing me to be your mother even though I was just a child myself. I know I made some mistakes along the way, but you have truly grown to be an amazing daughter, wife, and mother to Reyah, Mimi's girl. You, DeAna, taught me the true meaning of unconditional love. To my second born, my son Theo Sewell, Jr. TJ you came into the world full force and you haven't slowed down since!! You make me laugh. You keep me grounded, and it's been the two of us for a while now. I thank you for continuing to be the best son a mother could ever want.

To my sisters, Shawanda, Acacia, and Jasmine. As the oldest I've always felt like a second mother to y'all. I thank you for allowing me to be a big sister even when you didn't want me to. Even though I messed up when attempting to comb your hair, you still loved me regardless. All of you hold a special place in my heart because we all share a unique bond. I am so proud of the women that you have become!

Lastly, I want to dedicate this book to someone I met a long time ago, but I lost sight of who she was. I've reconnected with her again! That person is me. I dedicate this book to myself because I deserve it! Through all of my life's tribulations and triumphs, I am learning to appreciate, support, encourage, motivate, and love myself!

Acknowledgements

First of all I would like to thank God. He gave me a gift to be able to tell a story through my words. He provided me with the strength that I would need to get me through some very challenging, life-changing circumstances, and He has continued to provide an opportunity for me to grow.

Second of all I would like to thank my amazing editor and Soror Amanda Chambers. Without your company, Divine Legacy Publishing, I probably would still be sitting on this book. You made this publishing process very smooth, and I'm looking forward to us working together for many more books!

I'd also like to thank another Soror, my website designer Samika Johnson. You are my Nemo!! (Inside joke) You saw my vision and brought it to life! You've done more than just design my website. You've pretty much done anything I've asked of you, and I appreciate that!!

To all of my Sorors of Sigma Gamma Rho Sorority, Inc., I acknowledge you and thank you for the support that you have given. Eta Tau made. Delta Lambda Sigma raised. To my award-winning Omicron Sigma Alumnae Chapter, I thank you for being true sisters since I first relocated to the Memphis area.

To my cover designer, Natalie Castillo, thanks for bringing my vision to life. We had some hiccups along the way, but in the end you did a great job!!

To the Nelson and Mikell family, thank you for the DNA that helped me to be all that I am. My personality, intellect, sense of humor, talent, and beautiful chocolate skin all came from a mixture of my paternal and maternal family.

To my Natchez family, thanks for being my family. We don't always talk or see each other but when we do it's on. So I thank all of my first cousins: Jeremy, Perez, Salise, Kendrick, Marvin (thanks for taking my poem and turning it into a hot track), Christie, Krystal, Ashley, India, DJ, and Mercedes. Special shout out to my uncle Donald for giving me a place to stay in my time of need, my stepdad Jerry, and my uncles Otis and Tommy.

To my cousin and namesake Shelita, thanks for everything!! You are really a sister, and we've shared so many times together (some we can never tell anyone about lol). You have always supported me in everything, and I love you for that. Thanks to your mother Pudding for all she's done, including feeding me and riding with my mom to visit me in Memphis.

Friends come and go, and friendships change and evolve, so I'd like to shout out all of my friends who have withstood the tests of time and change. You know who you are, and I thank you so much for your support over the years!!

To the class of '94 Natchez High Bulldogs, y'all have been so supportive since knowing about me publishing this book! Thanks to all of you!

To my son's father, Theo Sewell, Sr., although we didn't work out, having you as such a great father to our son has helped me to be able to finish this book because I know that you're going to always make sure that he's good.

To my Memphis peeps, thanks for embracing me and helping to make Memphis my new home. Your unwavering support in so many ways is not taken for granted.

I didn't want to list names because there are so many people who have been with me on this journey! So if you know that you've supported me, encouraged me through your actions, words, thoughts, or prayers then I thank you!!

To my Milk and Cookies Crew, you girls have become so special to me!!! I'm so glad that the universe allowed our paths to cross because you have truly become my sisters in many ways!!

Last but certainty not least, I have to thank you Sir. Mr. LQT, I thank God for bringing you into my life!! You came at a time when I truly needed the support, the encouragement, and the motivation that you have given me. You have helped ensure that I met every deadline and at the same time you've shown me that I deserve to be spoiled and treated well! You have truly helped me to live up to my potential of being the best Shelia that I can be!! I'm so grateful to you for that!!

Meet Rico's Girls . . .

Sheree Maxwell, the outspoken teacher, deals with a present-day dilemma and a blast from the past that both threaten to expose a painful secret that Sheree has kept from everyone, including her girls.

Shaina Ferber, the unhappily married stay at home mom, has always been the envy of many who feel that she's very fortunate to be married to a wealthy businessman and being afforded with an excess of material things. This "expensive" lifestyle has come at the expense of Shaina's sense of self and independence and left her longing to prove that she's more than a wife and mother. This leads her to a secret decision that could result in gaining her independence but losing her marriage and friendships.

Morgan Cunningham, the career-driven attorney, has been so focused on her career and her family that she now feels that she is watching her life pass her by. Ready and open to new beginnings, Morgan is willing to shed her old life in more ways than one and walk into newness. But then a chance encounter leaves her with a devastating secret that could destroy her life as she knows it forever.

Maven James, the bonafide hood girl turned business owner, exudes a tough exterior but on the inside, she's just a broken little girl who still desires the love of a mother who has never been there for her. A new employee and an old flame enter her life, and they both bring secrets that could not only shatter her heart, but also put her on a different, unexpected path.

Chapter One

Sheree

"A good man is hard to find. Good sex is hard to leave."

I never thought that mess to be true until I found myself in the situation that I'm in now. Take me. I'm a thirty-nine year old professional, a teacher. Been teaching for sixteen years. I'm buying, yes I said buying, a four bedroom, two full bathrooms, spacious thirty-five hundred, eighty seven square feet brick home in an up and coming upscale neighborhood for young professionals like myself. I come from a good family. Well, an okay family. We have the occasional wife beater, cheater, drug dealer, and user, but doesn't every family?

I'm beautiful. Beautiful dark chocolate skin. Beautiful brown eyes with long lashes. Beautiful locs that I keep tight courtesy of my girl Maven. I'm sexy as hell. Most brothers, and even some sisters, call me "thick". Why? This luscious booty of course. I must admit, my butt is nice. I guess it is a little big. I mean, I have caused a few accidents when I'm jogging. But hey, like my aunt used to say, "If you got it, flaunt it. Make somebody else want it." So I flaunt it every chance I get. Well, enough about my booty. I'm also funny. I keep my co-workers, family, friends, and even strangers laughing all the time. I'm also smart, churchgoing, and creative. To put it simply, I got it going on baby! So why can't I let go? I know why. I'm not in love with Tyrell, but I am in lust with him. Okay. I said it. I'm addicted. That man does things to my body that I didn't know were possible. Trust me. He knows it too.

Tyrell Lamar Howard. Medium build and sexy as hell. Those damn eyes! One glance at them and your panties just fall down to the floor. He also has a deep Barry White like voice. I fell in love the moment I heard it. On top of that his "big little brother" is just delicious. Finger licking good like a piece of Kentucky Fried Chicken. If it wasn't for the sex, I would've kicked him to the curb when I found out he cheated on me the first time. Or maybe when he lied to me about having a job. Or how about when he took my cell phone and wouldn't return it even though he was the one who was cheating. But his "big little brother" is so good that it keeps me coming back. I've tried. I've tried putting Tyrell out. That didn't work. I even tried being celibate. That was a joke. I've gots to get mine. I've tried seeing someone else, but that didn't work. Probably because that fool Marshall couldn't last for more than five minutes. Unless of course I was giving his "member" a WMM.

You know, a warm mouth massage. Then his ass could last all night.

But back to Tyrell. He just can't seem to get it together. He's been to jail twice, once for four months and then for eight months. Like a damn fool, I was writing letters, sending boxes, and putting money on his books. At least I wasn't stupid enough to marry him like he wanted. Hell, even I wasn't going for that. No conjugal visits for me, not that I didn't get a little sumthing sumthing on the side. I took a personal day from school just so that I could be there to pick his sorry ass up from jail. I let him come back even after I saw my 2013 Chevy Avalanche parked at another heifer's house. Why? I've already said it. I'm addicted to him. And trust me, he knows it. He always rides around in my truck listening to that old Young Buck song. The one where the girl is singing, "Time and time I try to leave, but I just can't seem to leave your ass alone." She's right. Every time I let him go that good sex keeps calling me back. So that's why I tell my friends, "A good man is hard to find. Good sex is hard to leave." But I've had it. If . . . no . . . when I leave Tyrell this time, it's going to be for good. I don't care how good the sex is; I deserve to be treated better than this.

Enough talk about Tyrell. It's Friday night. Time to leave home and head to my weekly meeting with my three best friends, Shaina, Maven, and Morgan. I'm always the last to arrive and Mrs. Punctual, Shaina, is always the first. I guess she should be. That trick has it made in the shade. Stay-at-home mother of one beautiful daughter and a sexy husband who spoils her ridiculously. She has her choice of luxury vehicles and a damn 6 bedroom, two-leveled home in the uppity neighborhood. She doesn't have anything to do all day, so she should always be the first one to get there and secure our table.

Let me quit talking about Shania's spoiled butt and finish getting dressed. You know I have got to look good. There might be some fine brothers in Rico's tonight. And you know a sister is always looking for a spare. My momma always said to keep a spare because you never know when one of your tires might go flat. That's one piece of advice that has come in handy many times.

Okay, one final check in the mirror. Can't forget my sterling silver hoop earrings. I feel naked without them. Now to add my chocolate mousse lip gloss to these luscious lips. Check the booty. Yep, it's still banging. Now let's see what these other heifers have been up to all week.

Chapter Two

Shaina

"Money can't buy you love. But it can buy you a lot of other nonsense."

Now where is Xavier? He knows that tonight is Friday, the night for me to meet with my girlfriends. This is the only time I get to breathe. I mean, my daughter, Lyric, is the love of my life. I simply adore her. Xavier and I tried for two years before we were finally able to conceive. It was a rough pregnancy; I was sick the entire time. I even spent the last two months on mandatory bed rest. I guess that's why I smothered Lyric so much when she was a baby. I didn't want her to leave my sight. Nanna Grace used to always tell me, "Girl. You're spoiling that baby. You're gonna wished you wouldn't have done that." Boy was she right. Lyric won't let me leave her sight. She's always calling, "Mommy! Mommy!" When she began crawling, she used to come into the bathroom while I was on the toilet. Lyric pays her dad no attention. Probably because he's always working late, like tonight. I sometimes wonder what he's doing at the dealership so late. Maybe . . . my thoughts were interrupted by the ringing of my phone. Before I answer, my gut is already telling me that Xavier is going to be late getting home once again.

"Hey baby. Are you on your way?" I sighed at his reply. "You know tonight is Friday, and you said you were going to watch Lyric so I could . . . huh? You have another client? But baby can't you let Allen handle it? This is the second time this week that you've bailed on us . . . okay. Okay. Look you don't have to yell. I'll call your mom or your sister. They did say that they wanted to spend some time with Lyric."

I just stare at the phone in disbelief as Xavier continues to explain why once again he wouldn't be home on time. "Yes, Xavier. I'm still here. Guess I'll see you later. Yeah. We're going to Rico's. Lyric will probably spend the night . . . so . . . maybe we can spend some quality time together. It's been almost two months baby, and I miss being with you. Okay. I love you too."

I don't know what's going on with my husband. He's been acting so strange lately. I know he's been tied up with the business. He's the owner of Ferber Motor Inc., the largest luxury automobile dealership in our area. He'd recently hired Allen because he wanted to spend more time with Lyric and me. However, he's been missing dinner frequently. Once last month, he didn't come home at all. He told me that he and the boys went out for drinks after work, and he was so drunk that he just stayed at his brother's house. I didn't point out that his brother lives 30 miles from our home. If he drove there, he could have just as easily driven home. I don't know what to believe anymore.

One day last week, I received a strange phone call. It was a woman claiming that she was the grandmother of Xavier's son and that she was trying to contact him regarding the child's mother who was critically sick and possibly dying. I was so stunned that I just held the phone. I was brought back when the woman asked if I was the cleaning lady or something. I informed the old biddy that I was Xavier's wife and the mother of his *only* child Lyric Xalier Ferber. I then took her name and number and promised her that, although she was certainly mistaken about Xavier fathering a child with her daughter, I would deliver the message to him as soon as he arrived home.

Of course when I confronted Xavier, he laughed at me and called me a fool for even entertaining the phone call. He promised that he had not been unfaithful to me since the last time, which was two years ago. When I asked him how he knew that this child wasn't conceived then, he assured me that he was careful and that he would never turn his back on his child. He then took the phone number, tore it up, and threw it in the trash. He told me that it was just somebody screwing with my mind. He said that he would call to find out what was going on. I wanted to ask how he was going to call if he had torn up the number, but I know Xavier better than he knows himself. Therefore, I knew that before he tore that number up he had programmed it into his iPhone. What he doesn't know is that I had also programmed it into mine. I'm not stupid. I know there is something going on. I just haven't worked up the nerve to call yet. Partly because I don't know what to say, or maybe because I'm afraid to let anything destroy this fantasy world that Xavier has created for us.

I mean all of my friends, especially Sheree, think that I have the perfect life. It does probably look that way if you're on the outside looking in. Yes, we have a beautiful home. Yes, we have a three-car garage with three almost brand new cars parked in it. Yes, I have a walk-in closet that is filled with Prada, DKNY, and Dolce & Gabbana. Yes, I own over one hundred pairs of shoes including Jimmy Choo and of course the red bottoms, Louboutin. No, I don't have to worry about having enough money to pay the bills. Hell, I just take the checkbook and the credit cards and use them as freely as I want. Yes, I'm gorgeous, with beautiful caramel skin and almond shaped brown eyes. My hair stays laid with the best 16-inch bundles. My nails are always done in my signature French manicure. My size eight body is curvy in all the right places. I'm the perfect wife to a rich man. But all of these things come with a price: my self-esteem, my freedom, my sense of being me. I spend many nights in my home alone. When Xavier drinks, he becomes a different person. Even violent sometimes. I've heard people say, "Money can't buy you love, but it can buy you a lot of other nonsense." That's the truth. Beneath all of the jewelry, designer purses, and fancy clothes, is there any love left for Xavier and me? I don't know. I remember a time when I used to love him. A time when he consumed my every waking thought and even my dreams. But now . . . my gut feeling tells me that he's being unfaithful again. So that's why I have a secret plan. Not even the girls know about this. I just need to-

"Mommy, mommy. Where you at?" I hear a little voice call.

"Right here sweetie. And that's where are you? How would you like to go to Grandma B's house?" I ask as Lyric wraps her arms around my right leg.

"Yeah!" she says excitedly. "I love Grandma B. Can I take my new Doc McStuffins movie and my iPad?"

"Yes sweetie. Now go get your backpack while Mommy finishes getting dressed."

Let's check the time. Ooh, I have an hour to get dressed and take Lyric to B's house. The girls know that I'm always the first one to arrive. And of course, Sheree is always last. It's not like the heifer has any kids or a real man to hold her back. She should be the first one

9

there. But she spends all of her time trying to dress to impress, so I need to look damn good tonight as well. Not that I'm trying to impress anybody, but maybe a couple of looks might make me feel better because Xavier rarely gives me a first or second glance these days. Maybe it's time to let him see that I've still got it. Like Sheree always says, "If you've got it, flaunt it. Make somebody else want it." And I still have it.

Okay. Where are my black strappy sandals? You can never go wrong with black. Plus it makes me look slim. I'm wearing my new black Prada scooped-neck dress. It's cut just low enough in the front to offer a hint of my ample cleavage, and it stops a little bit below my knees. I think the girls will be proud since they're always teasing me about dressing like a married mother. News flash: that's what I am. But maybe tonight, I can pretend to be someone else.

"Lyric. Are you ready?" I call out to her.

"Yes ma'am. I'm ready to see Grandma B!!!"

"Okay. Let's go. You can call your daddy when you get there."

"Okay Mommy."

Chapter Three

Maven

"Some people are in your life for a reason, some for a season, and some just to get on your damn nerves."

"Maven, sweetie. Could you curl this little piece at the back? And then I want you to change this part. Now chile you know I likes my part on the right, not the left. And could you-"

"Okay Ms. Clara, I got ya," I hope she can't hear the agitation in my voice. "I just thought you might wanna try something new and different today. Might see a nice old man at the bingo hall."

"Chile. Hush your mouth. You know Wilbur was my one true love. No one can ever take his place. Did I tell you about the time Wilbur thought I was steppin' out on him with the milkman? All 'cause of that-"

"Nosey old biddy Ms. Staples," I finish for her. "Yes ma'am. You've told it to me before."

"You know Ms. Clara, you've been coming to Head to Toes since we've been opened," I say to Ms.

Clara as I pretended to fix a stray curl in the back of her head.

"I know. Was the first customer," she replies.

"Yeah. And the only one who still gets on my nerves."

"That's right chile," she says with pride. "Somebody gotta keep you in line. Since your own mama show ain't."

"Alright Ms. Clara. You're all done. I'll see you next week. Stop at Shaneice's desk, and she'll put you down for a wash, set, and color."

"Alright," she says as she gathers her things. "Y'all going to Rico's tonight?"

"Yes ma'am, as soon as I finish here. I gotta have a talk with one of the stylists. She's been fuc-messing up and missing work a lot lately. Probably have to let her go."

"Well alright sweetie. Have a good weekend. Gotta get to the bingo hall before Mrs. Jenkins. She always gets the best seats and cards."

"Bye Ms. Clara."

Whew! I look in the mirror and see that my burgundy hair is still perfectly coifed. I like the burgundy, but I think I might go blue soon. Blue always looks good next to my pecan tan complexion. My hair might be perfect but my brown eyes look tired. Ms. Clara has clearly worn me out. Glad to get her out of my chair. Don't get me wrong, I love Ms. Clara. Like I said, she's been coming here since we opened, so that's nine and a half years now. But she still manages to get on my damn nerves. She doesn't have enough hair to cover a tennis ball, yet she's always complaining about this curl and that damn part. I've been trying to get her to go natural and just cut that little bird's nest, but she refuses, saying if God wanted me to be bald, he would've made me an eagle. That woman, I tell ya. She-

"Maven! Tracy said you needed to see me!" A loud voice interrupts my thoughts. I look up to see Maiwaina switching her hips as she sashays into my office yelling like the hood rat that she is.

"Good evening to you too Maiwaina. Yes, I do. Give me just one second to -"

"Look!" she says with too much damn oomph in her voice. "I don't have all damn day! I need to get downtown by 8:00 so I can catch the mall. Gotta get a new outfit for the club tonight. So???"

Oh no she didn't. I know this little trick didn't have the nerve to get short with me. Her trifling behind has been late every day, and now she has the gall to try to get out of closing.

"Okay Maiwaina, since you're in such a hurry, I'll make this short and sweet so that your simple mind can understand. You've been late every day this week. You call in at least once every weekend."

"That's because-"

"And you have the nerve to parade your hood rat friends and boyfriends in here to get their hair braided for free. Read my big lips. You. Are. Fired," I say, emphasizing my words so they are clear.

"Now Ms. Maven, I'm sorry. It won't happen again."

"Clean out your locker and your styling section. We'll mail you your last check minus what you owe us for the free hairstyles."

"Fine," she turns and starts walking away :I don't need this anyway, Ms. BougieGhetto. I'm the best hair braider in this dump that you call a salon. Maiwaina means "hair braiding queen" in Nigeria. I come from a long line of hair braiding women!"

"Girl please," I laugh and walk out behind her. "Maiwaina probably means marijuana. Your momma just didn't know how to spell it. Now if you'll excuse me, Rico's famous strawberry-lime frozen margarita is calling my name," I say, dismissing her. I stop at the receptionist's desk. "Shawneice, if Ms. Hair braiding

Queen is not out of here in fifteen minutes, call security. I'm leaving. Make sure Cash knows he's opening in the morning. Tell him to be here at 7:00 a.m. sharp. You know we have that bridal party coming in tomorrow. See you in the a.m."

"Bye Ms. Maven," Shawneice says, clearly enjoying Maiwaina getting told off. "Have enough fun for me. Remind Ms. Shaina that her appointment is at 3:30."

Chapter Four

Morgan

"Sometimes loving everyone else too much can cause you to love yourself too little."

The phone ringing startled me out of my thoughts. I grab it and see that it's my niece, Niecey.

"Hello?"

"Hey Aunt Morgan."

"Hey Niecey. What's up?"

"Well, I hate to bother you," she says hesitantly. "But I need a ride."

"A ride? Where are you?"

"I'm still at school. I had detention for being late again, and I had a meeting with the yearbook committee," she explains. "Mama was supposed to pick me up at 4:30."

I count to ten as I try to calm myself. This is nothing new. My sister is always acting like Niecey should be somebody else's responsibility.

"Girl! It's almost 6:00!! You mean to tell me that you've been waiting outside at that school for more than an hour? Why didn't you call me earlier?"

"I tried about five times already, but it kept going straight to your voicemail. Plus Tish told us to quit calling you all the time." she says, referring to her mother by her first name.

"I don't give a damn what Tish said! If you ever need anything, you call me. Did you try calling Tish?"

"Yes ma'am. Jay said she left the house about three hours ago."

"Hell! Y'all only live about thirty minutes from the school. Okay. Give me about fifteen minutes, and I'll be there." I say just as I hear a horn honk through the phone.

"Niecey, get your ass of that damn phone and come on here," I hear my sister demand. "I gotta pick Larry up from work."

"Aunt Morgan that's okay. She just pulled up."

"Put her on the phone," I request and then hear the phone being passed.

"Hello?" Tish says, clearly agitated.

"Tish what in the hell is wrong with you leaving that girl at that school for more than an hour?"

"Look, Mo. I ain't got time for your b.s. today. I gotta pick up Larry from work, and I can't be late."

"So, let me get this straight," I say, my frustration getting the best of me. "It's okay for you to leave your sixteen year old daughter at school for over an hour, but you can't be late picking up your boyfriend? Girl, you are a damn fool."

"Look Morgan, I don't have time for or need your holier than thou attitude. Niecey is sixteen years old. Almost a damn woman. She's aight," she says, trying to dismiss me.

"Sixteen doesn't make you grown Tish," I fire back. "That's your problem. You've always treated Niecey like she's grown. She's still a child. You need to let her be one. She's more of a mother to Kadina and Jay than you are."

"Look uppity Ann, that's why I told them to stop calling you. You always got to put me down like you're perfect or something. Those are my damn kids, and I'll raise them how I want to! Now goodbye. Larry is waiting."

"Wait! Put Niecey back on the phone," I request.

"Niecey get this damn phone and get in the car!" Tish demands and I hear the phone being passed again.

"Yeah Auntie Mo."

"Look. You know how your momma is. She doesn't like me to do anything for you, but if you ever need anything don't hesitate to call me," I tell her.

"Yes ma'am. I'll remember that," she promised.

"Do you have any money for the weekend?"

"Nah, but it doesn't matter. Tish never lets me go anywhere. She's always gone with Larry. So I'll just be at the house all weekend," she explains and I can hear the sadness in her voice.

"Look, how about I come get you in the morning? I know this is Jay and Kadina's weekend to spend with their daddies. So you can spend the night with me and invite a couple of your friends for a sleepover. No boys."

"Ooh for real, Auntie Mo? That's cool! I'll call my friends as soon as I get home." Her voice perks up and I'm glad.

"Okay. I love you Niecey. I'm going to Rico's with my girls tonight, but call if you need me. Bye," I say and then hang up.

That damn sister of mine can be so trifling sometimes. She cares more about that hood ass boyfriend of hers than she does her own daughter. Probably because Niecey looks so much like her daddy, who Tish can't stand because he finally left her. She has never gotten over him. It's like she's punishing Niecey for what her daddy did. And me. I might as well take Niecey home with me. She is my heart, and I've always spoiled her as if she was mine. She's the daughter that I've always wanted but won't likely have. My doctor told me that I only have about a thirty to thirty-five percent chance of conceiving a child of my own, thanks to my Uncle Charles, but that's another story that I'm not ready to talk about yet.

I'm a family law attorney at the top firm in the city, and between that and my dependent family, I don't even have time for a baby. Hell right now, there's not a man in my life who is close to being father material. I do get sad sometimes, especially when I see Shaina with that precious Lyric, but I'm only thirty-eight. Even though Dr. Carson says that my chances of conceiving are dwindling every time I add a candle to my birthday cake, my biological clock still has a couple of ticks left.

Dang. It's almost 6:30. I look in the mirror hanging on the wall behind my desk. My thick, black natural hair is in holding its blowout well my make up hasn't budged since this morning when I applied it. I really do wear earth tones very well; they compliment my mocha skin and dark brown eyes. Content with my appearance, I grab my things and head toward my administrative assistant's desk.

"MariCruz, I'm gone for the evening. Please don't forget to put the Daris folder back on my desk before you leave," I tell her.

"No problem Ms. Morgan. I guess you're headed to Rico's for ladies night?" she asks.

"You know it MariCruz. You need to join us one night."

"I will but not tonight. I got a hot date." The smile on her face lets me know she's looking forward to it.

"Another one?"

"Yes ma'am. Sista gotta get laid."

"Don't you mean paid? Well . . . maybe both," I say as MariCruz and I both fall into hysterical bouts of laughter.

"MariCruz, you are one crazy chica. Have fun and be safe."

"I will. You too chica. Adios."

"Bye." I say as I look at my watch. 6:45. Okay, I have fifteen minutes to get to Rico's. Thank God I'm already uptown. That goody-two shoes Shaina is probably already there twiddling her thumbs, so I know I don't have to worry about finding a table.

Chapter Five

Shaina

"Surround yourself with friends who have their own problems. Then maybe you won't focus so much on your own."

As usual, I'm the first one to get here. Rico's is really jumping tonight. I'm glad I called ahead to make reservations. It's not like I needed to call; they always have a table reserved for us. We've been meeting at Rico's every Friday for the last five years. Sometimes it might just be two of us, but we're here no matter what. I look forward to these Friday nights. Especially lately since Xavier has been so busy.

"Hi Ms. Shaina," Christopher, the best host at Rico's, says as I walk in.

"Hi Christopher. I know you have our table ready, right?"

"Now Ms. Thang, I know you didn't go there," Christopher says and puts his hand on his hip as if he is about to read me my rights. "Don't I always have a spot for you and your hussy friends?"

I raise my eyebrows at Christopher and sternly say to him, "Hey! Now you've crossed the line. You know Sheree is the only hussy!"

We both break into a fit of giggles.

"Ooh Ms. Thang you are wrong, but you're so right. And before you ask, yes your favorite waiter, Ahmad, is here," he informs me with a wink.

"I wasn't going to-" I begin to explain before Christopher interrupts me.

"Save it girlfriend. I see the way the two of you look at each other every Friday night. Undressing each other with your eyes." Of course this fool Christopher has to "show" me how he thinks I look at Ahmad.

I flutter a little as I try to refute Christopher's accusations. "We don't look."

Christopher dismisses me with a wave of his hand. "Oh yes you do. I understand though. Boyfriend is fiiineee with a capital F. And don't worry, he's not gay. I already tried."

"Chris, you are a hot mess. Maybe he just didn't want you. Ever thought about that?"

"But I know somebody who does," Christopher mumbles under his breath as we head to the table.

I don't even ask Christopher to whom he was referring. As long as he isn't talking about my man, I'm good.

"Okay ma'am, here is your table. Your lover - I mean your waiter - Ahmad, will be with you, or in you, shortly," Christopher says with a devilish grin.

I slap him on his butt as he sashays away from the table. He might be a hot mess, but he's right about one thing. Ahmad is FINE. Gorgeous. Six feet three inches tall, sexy hazel brown eyes, and under that simple black uniform shirt and those black uniform pants, I know there's a great body. Probably rock hard abs with the little cut like D' Angelo in that "How Does it Feel" video. Mmm. That Ahmad is just scrumptious. I wonder how he looks naked.

Clearing his throat, Ahmad announces his presence at the table.

"Hi Ms. Shaina."

I can barely look up at him, especially after the erotic thoughts that I was just having about him. I manage to pull it together, though. Can't let him know how he really affects me. Well, not now anyway.

"Hi Ahmad."

"What can I get you to drink? Wait, I already know. An apple martini with, four ice cubes and two slices of apple."

"Ahmad, you are so efficient. That's why I love you."

Ahmad leans down and all six feet three inches of him look me squarely in my eyes. He whispers, "You love me Ms. Shaina?"

"I. Well. You know what I mean." I fumble over my words because I can't believe that I had actually said that to Ahmad!

Ahmad isn't buying it because he's still leaning down and looking at me with those sexy hazel eyes.

"How about you tell me what you mean, Ms. Shaina."

Before I can respond, Morgan appears at the table. Well, actually she's just there, and I don't know how long she had been standing there. I was too focused on the hazel-eyed beast in front of me.

"Am I interrupting something?" she asks with a smirk on her face.

"Hey Morgan. And what could you possibly be interrupting? Sit yourself down."

"Hello Ahmad. You already know what I want," she says as she settles herself at the table.

"Yes Ms. Morgan. You want a vodka tonic with a slice of lemon and no ice. Okay ladies, I'm going to get your drinks."

I know that as soon as Ahmad gets five steps from the table, Morgan will start with the third degree. Coming in 3. 2. 1.

"So, Ms. Thang, seems like somebody has a little fling going on with Mr. Ahmad."

Although my heart is racing at just the thought of a fling with Ahmad, I steady my voice as I not too convincingly tell Morgan, "What? Ahmad and I? A fling? Girl no. Xavier is all the man that I need."

"Okay Whitney freakin' Houston. I saw the way that you looked at him when he walked away to get our drinks. You might as well had stripped him of his uniform."

Why can't the other girls show up now, so I don't have to deal with Morgan and her ninety-nine questions?

"I wasn't looking at him," I insist.

"Un-huh." She's clearly not buying it. "So you haven't noticed how great his butt is?"

"Well, maybe a little," I admitted with a smile.

That's all the encouragement that Morgan needed. "I knew you were a little slutty housewife."

"Please. Don't you have to be having lots of sex with different people to be called a slut? I'm not even having sex with my own husband." Shucks. I didn't plan on revealing this information to anyone just yet. It was just too embarrassing.

"Shaina, what do you mean?" Morgan asks, her confusion clear. "I know you and that fine husband of yours are screwing all over that big monstrosity that you call a house."

"I wish. Xavier has been so busy lately that he hasn't touched me in over two months." I hate to admit this to Morgan, but it's the ugly truth. My sex life is pretty much nonexistent, except for the occasional release I get from pleasuring myself. I shouldn't have to do that unless I want to. Not because my husband is ignoring me.

I can tell Morgan is trying to choose her words carefully, which never works because she shoots from the hip anyway. She tells it to you straight; that's one of the reasons why I love her so much.

"Damn, Shaina," she starts. "See, that's why I don't want a damn husband. The sex seems to stop once you say, 'I do'."

"If you only knew Mo. I mean, I love Xavier, but lately I've been feeling like he's cheating. Again," I admit with a sigh.

"Well Shaina, you know I'm not the one to be giving advice on men to anybody. Hell, I haven't seen a man in my bedroom since the man came to install my Direct TV system." We both laugh at that because it's been over seven months since Morgan got her Direct TV system installed.

"We've got to do something about that Mo, but sometimes I wish I was you, Sheree, or Maven. Anybody except for a housewife."

"Heifer please. I wish I were you. You have a handsome, sexy husband and a beautiful home. Hell, your damn closet is bigger than some folks' whole bedrooms," she says with her hands raised up and out.

"I know all of that Mo, but all of that stuff is material. And you have a gorgeous home too. That you're buying. On your own. Without a man." I notice a look in Morgan's eyes that I've never seen before.

"That's all true, Shaina," she finally says. However, I'm lonely. Forget the husband, I just want a baby. Someone who will love me unconditionally. That won't expect me to bail them out. I'll do it because I have to do it."

"Girl, I know what you're saying. Life is so hard sometimes. I never realized that you wanted a baby so much."

"I know. I never really talk about it to anyone. I just think that maybe this empty space in my heart will be filled, you know?" The sadness in her eyes is evident.

"Aww Mo," I say and reach over to squeeze her hand. "If it's meant for you to be a mom, you will. But you're missing a key ingredient."

"What is that?"

"Some penis," I say matter-of-factly. That brings us to tears of laughter and helps to shift the mood to something less miserable then my lack of sex from my husband to Morgan needing sex to make a baby that she so desires.

"Ha. Ha. Very funny," she says as she wipes the tears from her eyes. "Well, I hope some penis comes along soon enough, because I'm not getting any younger."

"Ladies, here are your drinks," a sexy voice interrupts us.

"Thanks Ahmad. As usual, Sheree and Maven are late, so come back in about 15 minutes." I can't help but smile as I speak to him. He just does something to me.

"Anything for you Ms. Shaina," Ahmad says and then saunteres away from our table. I don't even try to hide this time as I watch him.

"Ooh girl!!l", Morgan shrieks.

"Whatever Mo. As I said, I am a happily married-"

"No sister," she interrupts. "You didn't say *happily* married."

"Well, Mo it doesn't matter. The point is I'm married, and even though my husband stepped outside of the marriage, I'm not going to do it."

"Okay okay, Shaina. I feel you, but can we at least agree on one thing?" she asks.

"What's that?"

"Ahmad is FINE!!!!"she exclaimes.

"No arguments here! I'll drink to that!!" and we raise our glasses in a toast.

Chapter Six

Maven

"Your happiness begins with you and the choices you're willing to make."

Damn! It's almost 6:30. I can't let Sheree get there before me. I would've been on my way if it wasn't for that damn Maiwaina. I can't believe she had the nerve to apologize and then get mad. That heifer! Now I gotta find a replacement for her trifling butt.

I guess that shouldn't be too hard. There's a beauty school uptown, but most of those heifers can't braid worth a penny. I would do better going back to the projects and getting some chick from there. I'm quite sure that a project chick won't mind getting paid under the table until I can get her in school and licensed. But going back to the projects means I might run into my trifling egg donor or any of my numerous half-brothers and sisters, cousins, or other relatives who think that me leaving the projects labels me as a sell-out. Well I'd rather be known as a sell-out than to resort to selling weed or even my body out of my apartment just to make ends meet.

Who in their right mind would stay in the projects when they have an opportunity to leave? I mean, if people only knew the things that happened to me in that place and how hard I'd worked to leave, they would understand why I refuse to go back. Hell, my mother is one of the many neighborhood crack whores, so what's left for me to go back to? All that would happen is that I would pass by my old apartment with the same broke drug dealers hanging out by the door and the hallway smelling like piss and weed. I'd climb the stairs all the way to the fifth floor only to find out that my mother is jail or in rehab. Again. Then, of course, I'd feel like a dummy for going back in the first place. I mean, the way I see it is I can't help mama if she doesn't want to be helped. So . . .

Damn, Rico's is packed tonight if the parking lot is any indication. Maybe I'll find myself a nice man in here tonight. Hell, he doesn't really have to be too nice. I'm just so horny that I'm craving some male attention. For some reason, lately, I've only been attracting younger men. I mean, I don't usually do the lil boy thing. That's more Sheree's speed. That heifer won't look at a man if he's not at least five years younger. But me? I like a man. A grown ass man. I just don't know if there's anything a young man could do for me. However, the way things are going, I might just have to try one. What's the worst that could happen? He could be married. He could be a liar, a cheater, or have crazy baby mamas. I've already been through all that with men my age and older. So, I don't think I have much to lose.

Good, I don't see Sheree's truck. Ha! That heifer is paying my tab tonight. She bet me that she would get to Rico's before me, and I'm definitely going to order the most expensive ish on the menu. She can afford to pay all of our tabs if she would stop taking care of that poor excuse of a man, Tyrell. But that's a whole other story. It's just that . . . Sheree is beautiful and fine as hell, as she always reminds us. She deserves better than Tyrell. For some reason she can't or won't get rid of him. Brother must got some good wood. Other than money, that's the only reason I can see a woman staying with a man like Tyrell. But who am I to talk? I don't have a man at all, just a bunch of numbers in my phone that I rarely use unless I need a "tune-up", and my body is telling me that it's time for one really soon. Like maybe tonight.

Finally a park. Guess I could stop being so cheap and valet park like everyone else. Or maybe I'll meet a young man tonight and he'll pay for me to valet park next Friday.

Dangit. Where is my purse? I hope I didn't leave it at the salon. I remember talking to Maiwaina. Then I told Shaneice to . . .yep, I left my purse in my office. Oh well. Sheree's paying tonight anyway, and I'm here almost every Friday, so I know they won't ask for my ID.

7:10. Well, I'm only 10 minutes late. Might as well go ahead and get this night started.

Chapter Seven

Sheree

"Everyone has a weakness. The difference is only if you give in to it or not."

Damn! It's already 7:15. That means I owe Maven dinner and drinks. The whole nine if she beat me to Rico's. Knowing that hussy, she was sure to be on time just so she wouldn't have to pay for anything tonight. I don't blame her because those were my plans too, and I would've beat her there if it wasn't for that damn Tyrell. Just as I was leaving the house, he called my phone telling me he was outside, and he just wanted to see me and get a kiss before I left for Rico's. Hell, I wanted to tell him to kiss my ass, but he's so nasty. He's never has a problem kissing me from head to toe without leaving a spot untouched. It's like he's an undercover porn star or something. There's no such thing as too freaky for Tyrell when it comes to our sexual "excursions" as I like to call them. His motto is, "How you know you ain't gonna like something if you don't try it?"

I guess he's right, but sometimes he's too much, even for me. Like tonight. He wanted me to get in his car and ride his big little brother. In the daytime. Knowing that neighbors might be out watering the grass, walking the dog, or just plain being nosey. But he kept saying, "Baby my tint is so dark, ain't nobody gonna see nothing." I wanted to say "Fool, I know how dark the tint is. Who did he think paid to get the windows tinted in the first place?" I kept that comment to myself because I knew that would've started another argument because he would say that I'm always quick to remind him of all that I have done for him . . . which over the past three years has been a lot. But Tyrell is not as dumb as he seems sometimes because he knows that his penis is my weakness. And when I climbed into the passenger seat of his car, he was already sitting there stroking it, all nine and a half inches . . . now you should understand why it's so hard for me to leave him. My center started throbbing, and I could feel a pool of wetness begin to form between my thighs, but if I let Tyrell know that, he would bend me over and I would never get to Rico's tonight. So, I did what I do best. I took that nine and a half inch beast and began to tame it with my mouth. I sucked and licked on him like he was a caramel lollipop, and I didn't stop until I got to his creamy center. Tyrell must have really enjoyed it because he just sat there rubbing my thighs saying, "Damn baby . . .damn". I know the power of my mouth so I gave Tyrell a quick hug, I didn't need his scent on me, and told him we would finish this after Rico's if I wasn't too drunk. I didn't give him a chance to respond before I climbed out of his car and walked back to the house to freshen up.

Now I have to wine and dine Maven's ass. I don't mind. Not really. Not because she can't afford it. She makes pretty good money at her salon. It's just that I feel sorry for her sometimes. She doesn't talk about it much, but I know she's bothered by her family, especially her mom. Maven doesn't even know where her mom is most of the time, and the only time her brothers and sisters come around is when they need some money or want their hair and nails hooked up, for free of course. So like I said, she can get a free ride this time, but I don't plan on letting her beat me to Rico's again. Next time, she will pay.

Damn, Rico's has a full house tonight. Thank God that I have a VIB . . . Very Irresistible Booty. You see, I always make sure that my VIB is on full display; I haven't paid for valet parking at Rico's since the girls and I made this our Friday night spot over five years ago. Which is a good thing because I wouldn't find a park tonight.

"Hey Sheree! You looking fine as hell tonight!!!" Marcus calls out from behind me as I step out of my car.

"Thanks Marcus. You know how I do," I reply.

"Yeah. I'll never forget how you do me. By the way, are we still hooking up later tonight?"

"Yes sweets. You know the routine."

"Aight. I will text you when I'm ready to leave. I can't wait to slide my tongue into your chocolate sweetness."

"She's all yours tonight baby. See you in a few."

Marcus is so cute, but he's such a baby. Only 28, but that baby has a grown man piece of wood. He's almost as good as Tyrell. One difference is I do love Tyrell. Marcus is just a quick lay when I need a different kinda itch scratched. Plus he doesn't come with any of the drama that Tyrell does; he's always at my beck and call whenever I need or just want him. But sometimes Marcus will say some foolishness like, "Sheree. You ready to be my boo?" I'm like little boy, I'm already somebody's boo.

I gotta start rationing this chocolate sweetness out to Marcus in small doses. I don't need him to get hooked. Although something in the back of my mind tells me it's already too late for that.

Chapter Eight

Morgan

"Sometimes you have to SUBTRACT things or people from your life so that you can in fact ADD to it."

As usual, I sit here and listen to Shaina complain about her husband. How he doesn't have sex with her, and how she thinks he's cheating on her again. I mean, I sometimes feel sorry for her. She is nice and will give her last to any of us, but at the same time, she knew that Xavier was no good when she first met him. We all did. The whole town tried to warn her that Xavier was a man-whore, but she didn't listen. I think that growing up in the "hood" as we all did, she just wanted someone to take care of her for a change. Not that I blame her. Hell, I completely understand. My family drives me damn crazy too. Especially my sister acting like a damn trifling man should come before her children. It's women like Tish that make me mad that I haven't been able to conceive yet. And now Shaina wants me to throw a pity party for her man. I don't think so. Not tonight. I have-

"Mo? Did you hear anything that I just said?" Shaina asked, interrupting my thoughts.

"I'm sorry Shaina. Thinking about the Daris case again," I lie as I try to bring my thoughts back to a happy place.

"Oh. How is that going?"

"Slowly. We're still waiting on the last report from our own psychologist," I explain.

"Oh......Well look who finally decided to join us. Hi, "Ms. Tardy for the Party," Shaina says, announcing Maven's arrival.

"Shaina, kiss my butt. One cheek at a time. Hey, Mo."

"Hey Maven. How are you this evening?"

"Girl. I'm fine now. Since Sheree hasn't made it yet, I get a free meal. And drinks!!!" she exclaims.

"You two are always betting when both of your arses are habitually late offenders!!" I remark as I look around for signs of Sheree's arrival.

"That's true, but I won tonight, and that's all that matters. Now Shaina where is your boy toy? I need to order my drink," Maven asks, looking around for Ahmad.

I know Maven's off the cuff comment is going to get a rise out of Shaina.

"First of all, Ahmad is not my boy toy. Second of all, he knows you are always late, so he should be back in about two to three minutes," Shaina responds.

"Look at Ms. Shaina. She knows *her* man's schedule," Maven responds sarcastically. "Anyway, what's been up ladies?"

I chose my words carefully before answering Maven because that nosey heifer always has a way of knowing when I'm holding back. "Well, it's been the same for me, Maven. Niecey and her mama driving me up the wall as usual."

"Now I know Tish is not still tripping. Then again she wouldn't be Tish is she wasn't bringing some drama to somebody's life." I'm relieved when she seems satisfied with my answer and moves on. "Shaina, how's my goddaughter?"

"Girl, she is great. Spending the night with her Grandma B tonight, so you know she's as good as gold."

"I hear you. Aw, here comes Ahmad," Maven says, wiggling her eyebrows at Shania suggestively.

"Hello Ms. Maven. What would you like this evening?" he asks when he reaches the table.

"Hey Ahmad. You remind me of a good bottle of wine; you just get better with time. I wonder if you taste just as delicious?" Maven boldly asks.

I think all of us, especially Shaina, anxiously await Ahmad's response to Maven's highly slutacious comment.

In his deep voice, he looks at Shaina, while he addresses Maven. "I don't know about all of that Ms. Maven. I've never tasted myself before, but I've been told that I'm pretty tasty."

Damn! Even my dormant hormones start to rise with that comment. I'm so glad that Maven decides to go ahead and order her drink.

"Okay Mr. Tasty, let me get a Cosmopolitan and a Ciroc with orange juice for Sheree."

"Yes ma'am. I'll be right back with your drink orders," he promises and then leaves.

"Um um um! Shaina, If you're not letting him knock you down, do you mind if he gives some to me?" Maven teases Shaina.

"Ha ha! Go for it Maven. As I was telling Morgan, I am a HAPPILY married woman." This heifer had the nerve to point at the 4-carat diamond ring on her left finger.

"And as I pointed out earlier, she said MARRIED, not HAPPILY married. And there is a difference," I reply quickly.

We all laugh because all of us knew the difference all too well.

"Hell, if you think about it ladies," I whisper as they all lean in to get closer to the foolishness that they know is about to spring from my mouth, "we're all married."

"Of course Shaina is HAPPILY married to her wonderful husband, Xavier. I'm married to Maria and the Daris case. Maven is married to "Head to Toes" including the staff and the clients. And-

"I'm married to my sexy damn self!!" Sheree proclaims as she comes to the table.

"Hey Sheree" we all manage to say amid laughter.

"Hey hoochies! And shut up Maven. I know I owe your wanting-something-free-so-I'll-beat-Sheree-to dinner ass," Sheree says as she sits down in her chair.

"Oh no heifer," Maven says pointing at Sheree. "You're not getting off that easy! I want dinner, drinks, and dessert!!!!"

Chapter Nine

Shaina

"It's all fun and games until the dose of medicine that you gave out is now making you sick."

Who would have thought that just over twelve hours ago I was having an engaging time with my three best friends? Our night together was just what I needed to help me forget the mundane existence that my life at home with Xavier had become.

As I enjoy my morning coffee, I can't help but think back to last night and what happened when I got home. Although Xavier and I haven't had sex in more than two months, looking at Ahmad's hot body for more than three hours had certainly ignited a fire in my nether regions that I hadn't felt in years. I was hoping that Xavier would be there to extinguish my flaming body with his "hose", but not so surprisingly, he brushed me off again reciting the phrase that had become all too familiar over the past two months, "I'm tired."

I just shrugged my shoulders, went to my armoire and found my silver bullet, and headed for the bathroom. Usually I would pleasure myself in one of the guest bathrooms because I didn't want Xavier to hear, but this time I didn't care. I wanted him to listen to the sounds that escaped from deep within my core. The sounds became almost animalistic as I imagined that Ahmad was serving me more than just drinks. And before I knew it, I had a release that was more intense than anything that Xavier and I shared over the course of our marriage. I guess the images of Ahmad standing behind me and thrusting his large manhood into me took me completely over the edge.

The last thing I remember before dozing off to sleep was thinking how it would be to wake up next to Ahmad every morning. I was completely spent when my thoughts of Ahmad were interrupted by Xavier rubbing against my backside; this was his way of letting me know that he wanted some of my attention. At that exact moment, I begin to feel nauseous. I don't know if it was the extra drinking that I did with the girls or the thought of Xavier inside of me, but I made a beeline to the bathroom to release the sickness from my belly.

"Hey, Sha, You alright in there?" Xavier yelled from our bedroom.

I pretended like I didn't hear him; I knew he was only concerned because he still thought that I was going to give him some. Well, I had news for him. It wasn't about to happen.

"Shaina?" Now Xavier hovered over me as I stood in front of the mirror brushing my teeth.

I just looked at him as if to say, "Don't you see that my mouth is full?"

Either he didn't see the ugly look that I gave him, or he didn't give a damn because that fool had the nerve to start to rub on his package and put his arms around my waist.

Now, I know that I'm supposed to be the nice, goody two-shoes one out of the group, but even I can't resist a jab or off the cuff comment once in a while.

So, I turned to face Xavier, put my hands on his chest, gazed all so lovingly into his green eyes, and sexily told him, "Xavier, I would love to remove all of my clothes until I'm as naked as the day I was born, climb into our massive bed, get onto all fours while I spread my cheeks and await the entrance of your hard thickness into my wet center, but . . . I'm tired."

With that, I turned and left Xavier standing in the restroom, mouth gaping wide as he watched me climb back into bed and pull the covers all the way over my head.

Chapter Ten

Morgan

"Just when you thought your life was all screwed up, someone always does or says something to let you know you're actually okay."

Ah heck. How could I forget to turn off this damn alarm?? It's still set for my weekday morning time of 6:00. I don't EVER wakeup before 9:00am on Saturdays unless I have an appointment at Head to Toes, but normally I just go in whenever I want. That's one of the benefits of being best friends with the owner. I call it having low friends in high places. Ha ha! I crack me up sometimes.

Whew! What a night last night! I mean we always have a great time at Rico's, but last night was epic. It started off with Sheree losing the bet to Maven for being late and supposing to pay for all of her drinks and dinner. However, the heifer Sheree left her purse at home after her little impromptu freak session with Tyrell, which meant that no-sex from husband Shaina had to pay for both of their meals. The better part is that since Shaina was mad with Xavier anyway, she decided to pay for my meal too!! Nothing like a free meal with no strings attached. The best part of the night was easily when we caught Shaina's boy toy, Ahmad, rubbing her shoulders as he helped her into her jacket. The rubbing of the shoulders wasn't as scandalous as the look in Shaina's eyes. She had "take me now" written all over her face. I knew she had a little slut in her!!

Speaking of slut, I need to call Maria to see how her hot date went last night. I grab my phone and hit her name on my favorites list.

"Hello?"

"Hey MariCruz."

"Oh hey Morgan," she responds with a hint of disappointment in her voice.

"Well good morning to you too chica," I say sarcastically as I realize MariCruz is expecting someone else.

"I'm sorry boss lady. I thought you were someone else."

"Yes, I can tell. I was calling to get the steamy details from your hot date with your mystery man last night."

"Well, sorry to tell you, but I have none. That punta stood me up!! I sat in that restaurant for more than an hour waiting on him to show up. He didn't even bother to text or call to tell me that he couldn't make it!!" MariCruz shouts and a string of Spanish expletives flew from her mouth.

"I'm sure he had a good reason MariCruz. Maybe something bad happened to him. Have you tried to call or go by his home to check?" I ask. She sounds so upset, and I feel bad for her.

"Yes, I've called and texted. Nothing. And I can't go by his home boss lady."

A sense of dread begins to fill the pit of my stomach. There's only one reason I can think of for why a woman can't go to the house of the man she's dating. I love MariCruz to death and would hate to see her in that kind of situation. But I need to know, so I ask har a question that I'm not so sure I want the answer to.

"Why can't you go by his home?"

"Please promise me that you won't judge me Morgan," she says and I can hear the worry in her voice.

"MariCruz, that's not my job. I'm a lawyer, not a judge."

"Okay." I hear her take a deep breath and exhale. I can't go to his house because . . . he's married."

Chapter Eleven

Sheree

"Losing trust in someone can take just a moment; gaining it back can take a lifetime."

Boy, boy, boy. About Last Night should've been made about me and my girls whenever we go to Rico's. As always, I had a blast. I even managed to have a quick session with Marcus. I just let him taste my Candy because I wasn't in the mood for anything more. Plus Marcus has been getting a little too clingy lately. Like that mess he tried to pull last night.

"Baby please come spend the night with me," Marcus practically begged.

"Marcus, you know we've already gone down this road before. I can't spend the night with you. I have a man at home, remember?" I asked.

"If you want to call him a man, you go right ahead, but you know that fool is just playing you Sheree. I'll treat you right if you just give me the chance," he promised.

In that moment, I didn't see Marcus as my cougar cub; I saw him as a GAM, a grown ass man, probably for the first time since knowing him. But I couldn't let him know that.

"Boy, you don't want me; you just want this Candy. But it's time for me to go. Thanks for kissing Candy. I'll hit you up tomorrow." I walked away before he could see how much his words had truly affected me. I mean, I knew that Tyrell was just using me, but it still hurt when someone else pointed it out to me.

As much as I hate to admit it, I sometimes wish that I could catch Tyrell doing something wrong to give me a reason to leave him. Not that I need another reason. He's given me plenty of reasons over the last three years, but I just don't want to be the one to end it. In my heart of hearts I know that it's only a matter of time because when you lose trust in someone it's hard to gain it back.

Enough of this mess with the men in my life. Time would work all of this out. For now, I need the man that was in my house to come service me this morning.

"Tyrell!!" No response. "Baby?"

Where the hell is this negro? Our house . . . my house is not that big that he can't hear me.

As I pick up my phone to call him, I remember that it's Saturday. Barbershop day. I'm still pissed, though, because he usually wakes me before he goes, which puts my mind into overdrive thinking of all the reasons that he chose to let me sleep in instead of waking me. I mean he usually wants a WMM, warm mouth massage, before he goes. What . . . wait a minute. I'm driving myself crazy probably for no reason. I mean, I should be glad that I didn't have to service him this morning, especially since I went to sleep with Marcus on my mind. Which really surprised me because I've sworn to myself that I won't take Marcus too seriously. My experience with most younger men is that they play way too many games, and I'm not just talking about Playstation and Xbox.

My friends and family have been telling me for years that I need to date older men. My response to that is always the same, "I like whoever likes me, and older men just don't seem that into me." Morgan believes that older men are intimidated by my booty. Maybe she's right, but as long as I'm still caught up with Tyrell, there's no point in me worrying about my booty, older men, or Marcus. My only concern is figuring out what the hell is going on with Tyrell this time and being prepared when everything is out in the open. My woman's intuition has never let me down before, and right now all signs are pointing to Tyrell being up to no good.

Chapter Twelve

Maven

"If you knew my story, then you'd want to read the rest of my book."

It's days like this that I'm so glad I'm my own boss. After an epic ladies' night at Rico's last night, there is no way that I could've gone to Heads to Toes at 7 o'clock this morning and be productive. Although I am very much hands on with my business, it does feel good to just lay in bed knowing that my staff is competent enough to make it without me. Well, at least for a few hours. My mind can't help but drift to thoughts of loneliness and feelings of being wanted and loved by a man. It's been too long since I've enjoyed any male companionship. I mean, it's not like I don't get plenty of interested admirers; it's just that I haven't found the one that I'm willing to totally give myself to. As horny as I am and as much as I just crave a man's touch, I want something more fulfilling than just a quick romp in the sheets. I—

Now, who would be calling me this early? I look down at my phone and see that it's the shop.

"Hello?

"Hey Maven, did I wake you?"

"You didn't. What's up Cash?"

"Are you coming in for this bridal party? We're kinda shorthanded."

"Damn! I forgot I had to fire Ms. Hairbraiding Queen. Give me about 30 minutes and I'll be there."

So much for feeling sorry about my love life or lack thereof. I have to get to the shop to do some Senegalese twist, and I have to make time today to find another hair braider. I need to spend my time working on finding another building to expand Heads to Toes, not servicing customers.

It has always been a dream of mine to be a boss in every sense of the word. Growing up in the projects and being the daughter of a drug addict taught me early on how to take care of myself. It also taught me that I never want to raise a family there, so I worked my ass off from the time I was in middle school up until now, and I have no plans on stopping anytime soon. I mean, I know that I don't have a family of my own now and, considering I'm still as single as a one dollar bill, that might be years down the line, but I still want to be prepared for when that time comes. I always vowed that my children would have everything that I didn't have as a child including loving parents, a stable home life, clean clothes, and food that didn't have to come from standing in line at the nearest food bank or stealing from the local grocery store.

The only thing standing in my way is having a man to be my husband and a father to my future children. If something doesn't shake soon, I'll have to think about other options. Because so many of my siblings ended up in the system, I never want to adopt or do foster care. I've always wanted to have my own biological children so that I can prove to myself that I'm nothing like my mother Gloria, and that I wouldn't just have a tribe of kids and just leave them to fend for themselves.

So I'll just continue to pray that a man will walk in my life soon, who can add on to all that I am already doing. Not take away from me as most of the men that I have dated in the past have done. And hopefully he'll come soon because not only am I getting lonely, but I'm well overdue for a tune-up.

Chapter Thirteen

Morgan

"You can't choose your family, but you can choose how you deal with them."

Between the epic time with the girls last night and the crazy phone call where MariCruz revealed that her hot date was in fact a married man, I need time to recover. The most wonderful thing about not having my own children was that I didn't have to listen to the pitter patter of little feet or feel a little body climbing onto my bed pleading for a bowl of cereal or a stack of hot pancakes. However, even before that last thought leaves my brain, it's replaced by another thought: the most awful thing about not having my own children is not having that one person who could give and receive love unconditionally. Which is something I feel like I've never had from my own mother.

I mean B.J. (short for Beverly Joe) was definitely not the worst mom. She often worked two and three jobs to make sure that Tish, my brother Jyron, and I had everything that we needed, but I never felt that close mother-daughter bond that I've seen with some of my female friends and their moms. At least not for me.

Now when it comes to Tish and Jyron, she always seems to smile just a little brighter and hug them just a little tighter than she ever does me.

For years, I didn't understand why I was treated differently, but then it dawned on me. It was because of my dad. I'm so alike him in many ways. I mean we're both dark-skinned. We're both lawyers, and we even share the same birth month. In fact, I'm born just one day after his birthday. Oh and how could I forget, I'm also named after my dad. Up until my mom was six months pregnant, they thought that she was carrying a boy. Hence my name, Morgan Danielle, and my father's name is Morgan Daniel.

I know that as a grown, successful woman I probably shouldn't be upset about how my mom treats me, but I'm still human. Although my dad always tells me "that's just the way BJ is," it still hurts. One of the reasons that I get so pissed at Tish is because she treats Niecey way differently than Kadina and Jay, all because she's still mad at Niecey's dad for leaving her and moving on with his life. It's like watching my mom raise my siblings and me all over again.

Speaking of siblings, I sure as hell didn't want to talk to Tish this morning, but I needed to remind her that I was letting Niecey spend the night at my house tonight.

"Hey, good morning Tish," I was trying to sound somewhat amicable and keep my composure since you never know what will set her off. Before I could utter another word, Tish rudely cut me off.

"Look Ms. I-wanna-be-a-mom-so-bad-that-I-try-to-take-over-my-niece-like-she's-mine". I already know you want her to spend the night, but she can't stay the night!!" I hold my phone away from my ear for a minute and just look at it, because I just can't believe that this trifling sister of mine is acting a fool this early in the morning.

"Look Tish. You are so wrong. You're only trying to punish me, but you're hurting Niecey too. Kadina and Jay are going with their daddies so why can't she come to my house tonight?"

Tish sucks her teeth before yelling, "See the point is Ms. Thang, you've got it all twisted! Niecey can't spend the night with you, but she can spend the rest of her life with you!"

What in the hell was up with my sis? I had to take a deep breath and count to ten before I addressed her again.

"The rest of her life? What do you possible mean by that Tish?" I ask incredulously, still trying to understand what she is saying.

I can hear the nastiness in Tish's voice when she say, "Just what I said! She can spend the rest of her life with you!"

"Since you want to always meddle in my business and tell me how to raise MY daughter, I'm gonna see how good of a mother you can be to her! When you come pick her up, make sure you come in your truck because she's bringing all of her stuff with her! Better yet, you're her NEW mommy, so you can buy your NEW daughter some NEW clothes, some NEW shoes, hell just buy her NEW everything!! From now on, you don't have to play mama, Niecey is all yours!!!"

Chapter Fourteen

Sheree

"What IS NOT said is sometimes more important than what IS said."

"Okay girl. I'll meet you at the salon. And try to calm yourself down before you go pick up Niecey. It's going to be a shame for the attorney to have to get bailed out of jail."

Well damn, was all I could say after hanging up the phone from talking to Morgan. I must say that in our more than twenty years of friendship, I have never heard her so upset. Take that back. She isn't upset; she is pissed!! She could barely calm down long enough to tell me the whole story, but I did piece together that Tish had decided that she wasn't going to be a mom to Niecey anymore. Who does that?!

As much as I want to lie in my big comfortable bed and worry about Morgan and her family drama, I have my own fish to fry. My man still hasn't returned home, but he did managed to send me a short text that read, "At the barbershop. Be home soon."

Now my mama didn't raise a fool. My gut tells me that Tyrell is up to no good again. When a person starts changing his or her routine, there is usually a reason why. At this point I just don't know if Tyrell's routine change is purely innocent or very salacious. My gut tells me that it is the latter, and my gut has never steered me in the wrong direction. So with that being said, I think it's time that I start to pay closer attention to my man because he usually tells me what I need to know without even opening his mouth.

See, the thing is, Tyrell and I have been a part of each other's lives in some capacity for so long that if I just zone in on his actions and his non-actions, I'll find out everything that I need to know or maybe what I don't want to know. I mean, don't get me wrong, he's done enough already for me to walk away from this relationship, but I guess I just don't want to think about starting over again at this age. I'm almost forty years young! At least I already know the type of shit that I'm going to deal with if I continue on with this relationship with Tyrell. On the other hand, I'm sick of the same old same old with dealing with him. Tyrell barely does enough to keep me interested, so I don't know why I'm having such a hard time letting him go.

I do know one thing, I have already told Tyrell that if I find any evidence of him being unfaithful again, whether it's a phone call, a text message, an email, or a damn smoke signal, I am skipping Plan A and going straight to Plan B - which is to be by myself.

I hear the slam of a car door, which means that Tyrell is back home. I hurry up and start getting dressed because if I don't he will most definitely be trying to "play", and until I find out what in the hell is going on with him, I'm rationing out my chocolate goodies to him.

"Where is my sexy Cocoa? You know I'm in love with that Cocoa," Tyrell half sings as he comes up behind me, pressing his big thighs and hardness into my booty.

"Hey baby. I was wondering if I was going to see you before I left to go to the salon," I murmur as I ease out of his embrace and sit on the bed to put on my shoes.

"I'm sorry bae. You know how it is at the barbershop on Saturday mornings."

"It's no problem baby. I needed the extra sleep this morning. We had quite a night last night at Rico's!" I reply back, turning to face him.

"Yes, I know. But there's something that I need to ask you. Who's Marcus?

Chapter Fifteen

Maven

"The only thing that's worse than failing is not even trying in the first place."

It's only 10:00am, and I am already bone tired. Although Maiwaina was a hood-rat, giving free braid styles away, trifling heifer, she was damn good at braiding hair. But not as good as me.

I've been braiding hair since I was eleven years old. All the chicks and most of the dudes in my projects would look me up to hook them up with the hottest braids design. There were times when I literally spent all day sitting on the front steps of the apartment complex serving client after client.

Hair braiding saved my life in many ways. For one, it kept me busy. So busy that I was able to escape the harsh reality of what was happening behind door #105A. No one knew that my mom overdosed and almost died on the living room three times. No one knew that many days we were without electricity and water because my mom spent the money getting high. No one knew that I spent many nights sleeping on a filthy mattress without any bedding because Mom would literally sell the sheets off of our beds and the clothes off of our backs just to get a fix. No one knew about the many nights that I had to fight off drug dealers because my mom tried to sell me to them just so she could stick a needle in her arm.

I was also able to use hair braiding to earn money that I used to not only purchase clothes and other necessities for myself, but also to help my ten brothers and sisters when they were still living in the home. Most of them were eventually placed with foster homes or taken by other family members. Last I heard, Glo, because I refuse to call her mom, was back in rehab after just giving birth to another child, number 12, who was immediately placed into foster care. It's such a damn shame that a woman like Glo, who used to be so vibrant and beautiful, could end up such a terrible, horrible, ugly inside and out, individual who had kids scattered across the city, state, and maybe even the country.

"Ms. Maven?" interrupts my thoughts as a smiling Cash appears at my office door. That little smirk on his face can only mean one of two things: there is a gorgeous woman needing to see me or there is a man, didn't matter if he was fine or not, who he thinks is there to sweep me off of my feet. Although I'm not in any hurry to date, I am interested to see what man has managed to put this goofy smirk on Cash's face.

"Um, Maven?" Cash repeats.

"Oh yes, Cash."

"There's a gentleman here to see you. He says he's interested in the barber position that he saw on our website."

Oh damn. I had forgotten all about that ad. Well, my hopes are dashed just a little bit since it seems I won't be meeting Mr. Right today. I still check the mirror and refresh my MAC cotton candy lip gloss. Hey, you never know. If he isn't interested, he might have a friend who would be. I walk out of my office, but I don't get far.

"Hi, Maven. I'm Karver," says a smooth chocolate voice.

"Hi, Karver. I'm Maven." I can barely finish my introduction as I look up into the greenest eyes I have ever seen. *Oh, Oh* I think to myself. This could be trouble with a capital T.

Chapter Sixteen

Shaina

"If you stay ready, you don't have to get ready."

I can't help but laugh every time I think about the look on Xavier's face when I turned down his offer for sex and told him I was tired. It may have been childish and a little petty, but considering the fact the Xavier hasn't been in the mood for sex in over two months, I feel justified.

I have taken so much disrespect and disloyalty from Xavier over the duration of our relationship, and I'm finally at a place in my life where I am ready to start living, really living, not just pretending that I'm happy in this big beautiful empty home, wearing all these designer clothes. None of those things really make me happy, but all of that is about to change.

I feel both nervous and excited about my plan. Especially since I haven't told any of the girls. I really want to confide in them, but all of them have so much drama in their own lives. Sheree is worrying about Tyrell cheating again, Maven has her hands full with Heads to Toes, and then I just found out that Morgan might be getting custody of Niecey. So I feel that my problems with Xavier are minimal compared to theirs, which leads to me get in my Mercedes E Class and drive downtown to the one place where I'm always welcomed, Rico's. And there's one person who is always available to talk and listen to me, Christopher. I mean even though Christopher is dramatic, he always has a way of making me look at things for what they really are. No matter how good, bad, or ugly it is; honestly at this moment, I need a dose of Christopher's no holds barred advice.

As I pull into the valet parking at Rico's, I take a deep breath. Today is going to be a deciding factor in how the rest of my life will go. No matter how horribly Xavier treated me in the past, I loved him. He was my first boyfriend and the only man who has ever seen me naked, besides the massage therapist. It's almost unimaginable to think about us not being together as a family, but I also know that I if I don't do something now, he will continue to treat me as just a woman and not his wife or the mother of his child.

A rap on my driver's side window shakes me from my thoughts of my life as it is now.

"Sorry. Here are my keys. Thanks," I mumble to the valet attendant as I grab my Gregory Sylvia bag, a birthday present from my husband, and walk to the doors of Rico's.

As I move closer to the hostess stand where Christopher usually prances around, my heart begins to beat a little faster, and I can't help but scan the room for Ahmad. Well, today must be my lucky day because before I can reach the hostess stand, Ahmad seems to magically appear before my eyes.

I can feel the hairs on the back of my neck stand up, and I manage to steady my voice before greeting him.

"Ahmad. Hi. What are you doing here? I mean, I know you work here,ut what are you doing here this early? Not that there's anything wrong with you being here early. It's just that I'm not used to seeing you here at this time," I stammer as I struggle to make any sense at all.

I couldn't believe how nervous Ahmad makes me. I look down at my shoes before I bring my attention back to Ahmad, who is clearly trying not to laugh.

"It's okay Ms. Shaina. To answer your question, well questions, today is actually my day off, so I decided to come by and let someone else serve me for a change since I'm usually the one who serves and pleases others," he explains.

Lord, this man could get me in some serious trouble. He actually sends chills up and down my spine with just his voice alone.

"Well, Ms. Shaina. I've told you why I'm here on a Saturday, and as much as I would love to be the reason that you chose to come back to Rico's after just being here last night, I don't think that's the case. Not this time anyway. So why are you here?"

Trying not to stare at his handsome face, I divulge, "I'm actually here to meet with Christopher."

"Well," Ahmad begins, "that's going to be hard to do considering that Christopher won't be back until next week. He and one of his sugar daddies went to Vegas."

"Oh no! That is this weekend!" I cry out. How could I forget that after Christopher had just reminded me last night? I guess in the words of Jamie Foxx, "blame it on the alcohol".

"It looks like I'm going to have to wait until Christopher returns from his vacation to speak with him. I guess I'll just head on to the salon early and wait for the other girls to get there," I decide out loud.

"Ms. Shaina? Do you believe in helping those that are in need? You know like doing charity work?" Ahmad asks as I'm preparing to walk away.

I give Ahmad a puzzled look before responding. "Uh, yes. I support several charitable organizations in the city."

Ahmad's next move catches me completely by surprise. He takes my hands, gazes into my eyes, and his voice seems to drop an octave when he drawls, "Ms. Shaina, today I am your charity case. I am in dire need of a beautiful woman to grace me with her presence and share stimulating conversation as we enjoy a delectable lunch and maybe dessert."

I can only nod my head to accept his invitation as Ahmad continues to hold on to my hand as he leads me down the steps, away from the crowded dining area and to a cozy table in the corner of the restaurant.

I can only pray as I hope that Ahmad can't hear the beating of my heart as he motions for a waitress to come and take our drink orders.

Chapter Seventeen

Maven

"There's a thin line between desperation and determination. Make sure you know the difference."

"Okay, Mr. Monroe, if everything clears with your background check, you can start as early as next Wednesday. In the meantime, I would suggest that you look over our employee handbook to familiarize yourself with the Heads to Toes way of conducting business. Do you have any questions?"

"Yes. I do. Could you give me the lead on some apartments close to the shop? I'm new in town, and I haven't been that successful on my own. Plus I'm tired of sleeping in hotels."

While listening to Karver speak, I can't help but notice how green his eyes are up close. It's like his eyes are looking into my soul.

"Um, yes" I stammer. "I can definitely help you with that. In fact, Pleasant Oaks, which is about a block from here, has a few vacancies. They're owned by one of my clients. If you can give me a few minutes, I'll call her."

"No problem. Thanks. If you don't mind, I'm going to go out here and talk with Cashir."

"Cash. We all just call him Cash. That's fine. I'll come and get you when I've finished speaking with Ms. Stephens." I watch as Karver walks out of my office and back to the front to find Cash.

Whew. I'm so glad that I got him out of my office. Something about those green eyes seemed hauntingly familiar to me. It's like I've met him before, but I know that I would remember him or at least his eyes.

I rack my brain trying to see if I had indeed met Karver before while I wait on Cheyenne to answer her phone.

"Hey Maven, how are you?" she asks

"Hey Cheyenne. I'm good girl. Look. I need a little favor from you. I have a potential new barber who is looking to rent an apartment, so of course I told him about you."

"What's he look like?"

"Cheyenne? What does how he looks have to do with anything? Besides, you're happily engaged, right?"

"I can look, can't I? No, I guess I shouldn't even do that if I'm trying to get married," she admitted.

"That's what I thought. Anyway, back to Karver. Do you have a unit for him or not?"

"Yes ma'am, I do."

Okay, thanks friend. I'll go get him now and send him over to you. Please be on your best behavior.

"He must be cute if you're asking for my best behavior," she teases.

"I didn't say he was cute!"

"Yup, he's cute."

You know what! Goodbye, Cheyenne!"

Damn, Cheyenne just wouldn't let up. She keeps asking me if he's cute. Was he fine? Is he married? I'm like damn I didn't interrogate the man; I just gave him an interview. I finally get her off that phone and gather myself before I page Karver back to my office. I can't help but smile when I notice his roughly 6'4 slender but muscular frame standing in my doorway.

"Come on in Karver," I call out to him.

"I'm assuming by that smile on your face that your friend has found my new home?"

I feel my cheeks filling with red. "Yes, she had. She's actually waiting on you now. I've written the address on the back of my business card."

"Thank you so much Maven. I really appreciate this. I do have one more question for you."

My ears perk up as I timidly answer, "Yes?"

"Can I take you out for dinner to show you my appreciation?"

Chapter Eighteen

Sheree

"If you give it the proper love and attention, the grass can be greener on the other side."

Oh my God. I'm so pissed right now! I can't believe that Marcus broke Rule #1: Never text me unless I have texted you first! He had texted my phone several times last night after I made it home asking was I okay and had I made it safely. That damn fool! He was acting like I had downed ten shots of vodka straight with no chasers when all I had was 2 or 3 maybe 4 drinks. Plus, I only live like ten minutes from Rico's. I know I should probably be happy or flattered that he was so concerned about me, but right now I'm not. Luckily I was able to calm Tyrell down by telling him that Marcus works at Rico's and that he always checks on all of us after we leave on Fridays. I don't know if he bought that or not, but once I wrapped my lips around his swollen manhood, it seemed as if those text messages from Marcus were the last thing on his mind.

Now I'm finally on my way to the salon to hang with the rest of the ladies and of course to get my locs washed, conditioned, and retwisted. But first, I need to call Marcus and set him straight about last night.

"Hey, my chocolate cake. I-" I cut him off before he could finish.

"Save the chocolate cake shit Marcus! Why in the hell did you text my phone like that last night?!!! You know the number 1 rule. Don't text me unless I text you first! You had Tyrell asking a million damn questions about you this morning!"

I pause with my verbal tongue lashing long enough to see what his young ass explanation will be.

"I'm sorry Sheree. I really was just checking on you. You and the rest of the ladies seemed to have had more than the usual fun last night. I really didn't think. I was just worried about you. That's all. Honestly."

As mad as I am at Marcus, my anger begins to dissipate. I can tell from his tone that he really was just concerned about me. For that, I'm actually thankful because lately Tyrell never seems to care where I am or when I get home.

"It's okay Marcus. I apologize for yelling at you. I'm just a little on edge right now."

"Care to talk about it babe?" Marcus asks in a way that made me want to pour out my heart to him.

"No. Well, not right now. But I know that if and when I'm ready, you'll be there for me. Right?

"Sheree? Don't you know by now that I'll always be here for you?"

Whenever Marcus says that, I never know how to respond. Part of me is pissed because I don't know if I believe him. I mean, all of the men in my life, beginning with my dad, have done nothing but betray me, use me, abuse me, or leave me. So when it comes to men, my heart has been hardened, which is why I have Marcus around in the first place.

I am always the loyal one in the relationship at first. When I'm in, I'm all in. When Tyrell and I were together for the first year or so, you couldn't have paid me to look at or talk to another man, let alone actually give my goodies to another man. However, all of that changed when he cheated the first time. So I told myself that never again would I allow a man to just do what the hell he wants to do in our relationship.

While I didn't know if Marcus's words were backed-up by genuine feelings, I was flattered that he seemed to truly want a permanent part in my life. After all, he was young, handsome, physically fit, intelligent, and goal-oriented. Many of the qualities that most women, including myself, would look for in a man.

There is one question burning my mind as I tell Marcus that I will hit him up later: Could it be possible that my appetizer can become my main course?

Chapter Nineteen

Morgan

"The first step in pouring love into the lives of others is to first pour love into your own life."

Lord knows my nightly prayers always include my desire to have a child, but I had no idea that meant I would become a parent overnight.

I really believed that when I got to my sister's apartment I would be able to calm her down and possibly talk some sense into her silly ass. Boy was I wrong. Tish was just as irrational in person as she had been on the phone. Then to make matters worse, my mom was there too, and of course as usual she fed into Tish's nonsense, telling me that I needed to be the bigger person and learn how to get along with Tish. In that moment, I realized that BJ was just as delusional as Tish if she thought that I was going to apologize. For what? For being a great aunt to my nieces and nephew. Or for loving others too much, which meant that I sometimes forget about myself? Or maybe I should apologize for turning out halfway decent despite the fact that my "mother" has never said "I love you" to me.

I wouldn't dare. So, as usual, I took the high road and literally bit my tongue to stop me from muttering a word to Tish or BJ.

"Auntie Mo?" Niecey's wavering voice pulls me back to the present moment, which is good since I;m driving.

"Yes sweetie?"

"Thank you for coming to get me".

My heart aches as I turn to look at the beautiful chocolate face of my usually high-spirited niece, who now looking like a very fragile and worried little girl.

"You don't have to thank me Niecey. As I have told you many times before, I love you as if you were my own. I'll do anything for you, and besides, I do get lonely in that big house of mine sometimes. Plus you could help me with the chores too," I joke to try to cheer her up. I'm glad to see that I manage to put a slight smile on Niecey's face.

"Well, I appreciate it Auntie. I really do."

"I know you do Niecey. Now you know I have to go to the salon to get my hair done. How about you get a wash and a nice roller set and maybe a mani and pedi?" I ask, already knowing the answer to this question.

"Ooh!! For real Auntie?" Niecey squeals as a grin begins to slowly cover her entire face.

"Yes, but I must warn you that being at the salon with the other ladies on a Saturday usually turns into an all-day affair. We will probably be there for a few hours," I explain.

"That's fine with me Auntie. I'm sure you'll let me borrow your iPad so that I can get on Instagram and Snapchat."

"What in the hell is Snapchat?" I ask Niecey.

Niecey can't hide her laughter. "OMG Auntie. I can't believe you've never heard of Snapchat! How about I show you how it works later? In the meantime can you please give me some music that I can jam to? This sounds like the music that they play in elevators!"

It's my turn to laugh as we make our way down the interstate towards the salon.

Chapter Twenty

Shaina

"A person will only do to you what you allow to be done."

I'm so glad that the girls are not with me right now! I think to myself as I wait for the Valet attendant at Rico's to bring my car.

There is no way that I can hide the pure bliss that I feel right now. Although I was initially hesitant to have lunch with Ahmad, I'm so glad that he really didn't give me a choice in the matter.

I learned so much about Ahmad that I probably wouldn't have learned from the brief conversations that came with seeing him on Friday nights. What I learned about Ahmad has given me a newfound sense of admiration and appreciation for him. I mean, I've always admired his body, but now I admire the man that he is. He's goal-oriented. I found out that working at Rico's is just a part-time gig for him. He is finishing up his Master's Degree, and he's also in the start-up phase of developing his own nonprofit organization for young men. I also learned that he is nurturing; he's helping to take care of his fifteen year old nephew whose mom had died in a car accident three years ago. I could tell how proud he is of this because his chest seemed to stick out just a little more when he spoke of how his nephew was a star football player at his high school.

Of course, hearing all of this while looking into his eyes and stealing glimpses of his hard biceps underneath his shirt made me think about Ahmad in a way that I never had before. But I did my best to hide my feelings because I didn't want to drag anyone else into the mess of a marriage that Xavier and I currently have.

Even while I was having lunch with Ahmad, I still couldn't help but reflect on all of the years that I had lived my life in Xavier's shadow. While I can blame him for the way that he's treated me over the years, I can't allow him to take all of the blame. I allowed Xavier to put me in a position where I was blinded by "things" instead of paying attention to what really mattered.

I know that most people, including some of my friends, feel that I don't have anything to complain about. I mean, considering some of the terrible, heart-breaking situations that my friends grew up in, I am very fortunate. I grew up with my mother and my father. They were high school sweethearts and are still married to this day. Even though my father worked for years as a postal carrier, we ended up living in a neighborhood that was right next door to the housing projects, which is how I met Sheree, Shaina, and Maven.

I always wondered why my dad never moved us to a better neighborhood considering that he made more than enough money to afford a home in a nicer part of the city. I would later learn that my dad was so complacent about staying there because my mom didn't work outside of the home, and he needed the money to support his one vice: women.

If I had known about my father's philandering ways when I was a young girl, I'm sure our relationship wouldn't be as close as it is now. While growing up I was always daddy's little girl. My dad could do no wrong in my eyes. He absolutely adored me and spoiled me to the dismay of my mother, who would often voice her disapproval that he was turning me into a brat. That never stopped my dad. I can honestly never remember a time when I asked for something and he told me no.

My dad always called me his little princess, and it was he who instilled in me that I deserved the best of everything. However, he also instilled in me that a woman's place is in the home and that her job is to please her husband and sacrifice her own dreams, goals, and aspirations for her husband's. That's what my mom did for my dad and still does to this day.

Sadly, I must admit that I've done the same thing. I put my dreams on the back burner in the name of being the perfect wife to Xavier and the perfect mother to Lyric. I can't complain to anyone because my friends all think that I'm the lucky one, and my mom will just remind me that being a good wife and mother is just what a woman is supposed to do. So for years, that's what I've done.

But now after my lunch "date" with Ahmad, I am more than ready to take back control of my life.

Chapter Twenty-One

Sheree

"If you don't want someone to tell your secrets, keep them to yourself."

As I pull up to the salon and try to find a parking space, I decide that I will leave the conversations with Tyrell and Marcus in the back of my mind. Besides, I can't wait to talk to the other girls to see if they have any news to share since last night.

As if she can read my mind, Shaina parks right next to me, and I can't help but notice that there is something different about her. I can't quite put my finger on it, but there is something going on with Ms. Thang, and I'm determined to try to get the four-one-one before or if she tells the others.

I roll down my passenger side window and call out to Shaina.

"Say ma, what yo name is?"

Shaina cracks a smile before responding, "My name is Nunya. None of your business. You are so crazy

Sheree. You know we left the projects to not have to deal with men trying to "holler" at us like that."

"I know, I know." I agree as Shaina climbs into the passenger side of my truck. I don't waste one second in giving Shaina the third degree.

"So, what is going on with you today, Ms. Thang?"

"Oh nothing. I just left Rico's," Shaina answers as she begins to twist her hair around her fingers.

Now, although I love of all the girls as my sisters, I must admit that Shaina has a very special place in my heart. When I first moved to the projects to live with my grandmother, Shaina was the first friend that I made even though she didn't actually live in the projects. All through middle school and in high school, when Morgan stopped hanging with us because of Xavier, and when Maven was too busy doing hair or looking for her mom after school, Shaina and I continued to blossom as friends. We typically spent weekends at each other's houses, rode the bus together, attended church together, and eventually became roommates in college . . . until she left to move in with Xavier, but that's another story for another day.

With that being said, I know Shaina. Whenever she starts twisting her hair around her fingers, she's usually hiding something. For example, when she finally became pregnant with Lyric, she twisted her hair around her fingers at least five Fridays at Rico's before she revealed to us that we were going to be aunties.

Knowing Shaina as well as I do, I know that when it comes to keeping secrets, she is like me. We'll hold on to a secret until we're sure that we want to share it. If she wants to play coy as if nothing was going on, I will humor her for now.

"Oh okay. Rico's? On a Saturday? Why?" I ask her.

Continuing to twist her hair around her fingers, Shaina looks away as she gives me a half-ass answer. "Oh, nothing. I went to go to lunch with that crazy Christopher, but I forgot that he was going to Vegas this weekend."

I can't help but smile because I think I already know what that means.

"So if you didn't have lunch with Christopher, what did you do?"

"Well, I didn't want to waste time going back home when I knew that I had to be here by 3:00, so I had a lunch date with Ahmad."

Chapter Twenty-Two

Morgan

"A smile or laughter costs nothing to give but can be priceless to receive."

What a day I've had already, and it's only 3:00pm!! Now that Niecey and I are pulling into Heads to Toes, I do feel a little of the pressure leaving my body. I can always count on my girls to listen to my problems, make me laugh, and maybe even help me forget all of my drama by sharing their own issues.

"Let's go Niecey, and before you ask, you can get the works today. Since I'm your NEW mama, you have to get the same treatment that your NEW mama does!!" I say in an exaggerated voice.

"Ooooh! Thanks Auntie Mo, I mean NEW mama! That does include a mani and a pedi, right?"

"Of course Niecey. I'm not like Tish; when I tell you something, it's exactly what I mean. You understand?" I ask.

"Yes mam. I understand," she says. I can see the hope in her eyes. "Come on Mama Auntie Mo. Let's go get hooked up!"

I can't help but laugh as Niecey and I walk arm in arm into the salon.

"Hey y'all! This is Niecey. She is getting full service today. Hair, nails, and feet. Be good to her!" I request when we enter.

"We got you Ms. Morgan. You already know that your crew is part of Maven's VIC." Cash replies, coming to get Niecey.

"Thanks" I say as I make my way to the back of the salon past Maven's office to the VIC section. Maven installed the VIC, Very Important Client, section about three years ago when she began to attract well-known clients and also clients with serious hair care issues like chemotherapy patients and those who suffer from alopecia and other hair loss conditions.

I personally love the VIC area because it has its own set of stylists, two personal massage therapists, and of course wine, champagne, and trays of appetizers.

I hear Sheree's loud cackle before I even walk through the doors.

"What in the hell is so funny in here?" I ask as I step into a room filled with laughter.

Maven stops laughing long enough to answer, "Girl, we were laughing at your club "girlfriend" from last night."

'That shit is not funny Maven. Hell, when the bartender said that a man had offered to buy us a drink, y'all all thought that she was a man too! So don't act like I'm the only one who was fooled!" I holler.

Sheree just has to put in her fifty cents. "Yeah, but she stood by your chair buying you drinks last night, not my chair. For which I must say thanks again. I hope she's there next week too!"

I join in the laughter too. "True, true. Nothing like being pimped out by your friends for drinks. Anyway there was that one guy who was kinda cute, but y'all already know that he was too damn small for me! Hell, my butt cheeks would eat him for dinner and still have room left for dessert!"

This really cracks all of the girls up because the one thing we all have in common is a big booty!

We are interrupted by a knock on the door. "Come in!" we all call out and the door opens.

A deep, baritone says, "Hi Ms. Maven. I just wanted to thank you for your help yesterday with the apartment. Hopefully, I'll see you on Wednesday. You ladies enjoy the rest of your evening."

We all watch as a tall, handsome stranger with green eyes walks back out of the door. All eyes turn to look at Maven with the same question on our lips, "Who was this caramel, green-eyed Adonis?"

Chapter Twenty-Three

Maven

"Don't play where you get your pay."

Boy, boy, boy! What a week this has been! I've had to deal with the girls continuing to question me about Karver's and mine non-existent relationship. No matter how many times I try to tell them that Karver is just my new barber, and I only went on one date with him because he wanted to show me appreciation for the job and the apartment, they don't believe me.

Don't get me wrong, it's not like I haven't thought about Karver as a potential date. I mean, he's very handsome with a great body. He's very intelligent, he goes to church regularly, and he has an amazing sense of humor. These are many of the qualities that I look for in a man. The only thing is that it's apparent to both Karver and me that we're not compatible as lovers. It was very clear when after our "date" Karver and I both leaned in to give each other a goodnight kiss. I was looking into his green eyes. He was looking into my brown eyes. Then all of a sudden, it happened. We both burst out laughing!! It was obvious then that we wouldn't be lovers, but we would be best friends from that moment on out.

When I'm around Karver, I mostly feel like one of his homeboys. We just don't connect on a romantic or sexual level. My "special place" doesn't react or tingle at all when I'm around him. Honestly, it's probably for the best. I mean, Karver does work for me, and I have one motto that I have never strayed away from, "I don't play where I get my pay." Who knows? Maybe I can introduce him to one of my clients or better yet, maybe Morgan would want to go out with him. Lord knows she needs a date as much as I do.

"Hey boss lady," Karver's deep voice interrupts my thoughts about him.

"Uh oh. Whenever I hear "boss lady" coming from one of my employees, I immediately ready myself for some type of crazy request. So, what's up Karver?"

"Nah. Nothing like that Maven," Karver declares as he tries his best to avoid looking at me, instead focusing his attention on a painting on my wall.

Something about his demeanor and the look on his face has me very concerned. Over the past week or so, Karver and I have spent damn near every day and most evenings together playing cards and dominoes, watching sports at a few of the hottest sports bars in town, or just talking about everything from politics to music. We even went to the gentleman's club. I actually like going to the strip club; don't judge me. A lot of the women there are clients of mine, and the strip club serves the best damn wings.

But for as much time as Karver and I have spent together, I still feel that there is so much that I didn't know about him. So I'm kind of taken aback by the way he was looking and acting right now.

"Karver, I know that we're really just getting to know each other, but I truly consider you one of my best friends, and I hope that you feel the same way about me. With that being said, I want you to know that you can tell me anything." I sincerely hope that Karver will open up to me because whatever is bothering him has to be something very serious.

I can see Karver take a deep breath as he walks over to my desk and takes a seat in one of the black leather chairs. "Maven I want you to know that I truly appreciate everything you've done for me from giving me a job, finding me a place to live, to showing me around, and even hanging out with me damn near every day since I've been here.

"Karver, you're scaring me! What the hell is going on with you?"

"Maven, you don't have to be scared of me, but I haven't been totally honest with you. I'm not who I say

I am," the look on his face is ominous and I feel dread start to creep up my spine.

"What do you mean?" When he doesn't answer quick enough, I say. "Look Karver, if you don't start explaining right now, then I'm going to call for security to toss your ass out of here!"

"Hold on Maven. Please just hear me out," he requests.

"Why should I Karver?"

"Because you just told me that I was your friend and that you would do anything for me. So as your friend, I'm asking you to hear me out. Please."

"Okay, but make it quick Karver. You're really scaring me," me heart is in my throat as I imagine the worst. Is he a murder? Rapist? Drug lord?

"When I say that I'm not who I say I am Maven, that's because I don't know who I am."

"What do you mean by that?"

"I don't know who I am because I was adopted when I was just four days old. I only found out last year when my dad became ill and begged my mom to tell me the truth," he explains.

"Oh Karver," I say as my heartbeats begin to return to normal. "I am so sorry to hear that. I know how you feel because my mom is an addict. I've never met my dad, and I also have many brothers and sisters who I've never met because they were adopted before they even left the hospital."

"Thanks," he said "I lied to you about was the reason that I moved here. I'm not here just because I needed to relocate or to get a job. I'm here because I need to find out about my past."

I can feel myself stepping into my around the way girl pose. Hands on hips and all as I stand up to look more clearly at Karver. "Your past?" I ask. "What happened in your past?"

"I need to find my birth mother."

Chapter Twenty-Four

Shaina

"If you can and you are grown, then you should work to have your own."

I twiddle my fingers as I wait for the results of my test. I haven't been this nervous in a long time. This test will be a determining factor in the next steps of my life. I couldn't believe that I had managed to keep this secret from the rest of the girls because I've shared every other major life event with them since I lost my virginity to Xavier in the 11th grade. However, time and life have taught me that sometimes it's just best to keep your secrets to yourself.

So I have, but after today they will know what I've been hiding from them for the past year.

"Mrs. Ferber?" the testing coordinator says and I stand to greet her.

"Hi Ms. Gully. I hope you have good news for me."

"Well yes, actually I do. You passed your test! You are now a certified event planner and coordinator!!" she says with excitement.

"Thank you so much Ms. Gully for all of your help! You don't know how much this means to me. I now feel like I can truly become an independent woman and be known as something more than just Xavier's wife and Lyric's mom," I lament as I begin to feel tears well up in the corners of my eyes.

Thank God!! I can now have my own identity apart from Xavier, and I can take control of my life and my destiny.

"That's so wonderful Shaina. Over this last year and a half I've watched you, and I always sensed that there was something special about you. Now I know that. I will tell you like I tell all other young women, including my daughter. If you can and you are grown, then you should work to have your own. What I mean by that is it doesn't matter how much money your husband makes, you should always have the means to take care of yourself in case something should happen. Now you'll be able to do that Shaina."

I can only nod my head and reach out to hug Ms. Gully. As she pulls my head to her chest, the tears begin to fall from my eyes. Being in her embrace reminds me of how my grandmother would hug me tight, except my grandmother often smelled of castor oil, fried chicken, and Benson and Hedges cigarettes.

I pull away from Ms. Gully and wipe my eyes.

"Ms. Gully, you are so right. I'm ready to walk into God's purpose and calling for my life and embrace my greatness!!" I proclaim as Ms. Gully beams proudly.

"That's my girl. Now, you know I want to be there when you plan your first big event."

"Oh Ms. Gully you already know you'll be invited and have a reserved seat at my VIP table. In fact, I've already planned it. You know how the girls and I have a big celebration for our birthdays? Well this year is no different except this year I'm planning the entire event!" I tell her excitedly.

"Well that's great, Shaina, but isn't that just two months away? How will you find a location that's big enough in this short amount of time?"

I couldn't help but smile as I prepare to reveal part of my secret to the first person. "Problem already solved Ms. Gully. I don't need to find a location because I already bought my own building." I pull out my iPad to show Ms. Gully my new investment.

"I present to you: Lyric's Loft!"

Chapter Twenty-Five

Sheree

"Appreciate who or what you HAVE before it becomes who or what you HAD."

I am so glad that my planning period is at the end of the day, because if I have to look at a child right now, I think I might slap the hell out of him or her.

This has been one hell of a week, both professionally and personally. At school, it is testing week, which always means that this is the time when students show their ass the most. I've had a fight-filled week, and it's not the students; two of my co-workers got into a fight over what else, a damn man. Now both of them are suspended for a week, which means that I have to carry their loads of duty and professional development too.

Then, on top of that, my principal is sending me to a mandatory workshop for three days next week in Atlanta. Now, I never mind going to Atlanta, but next week is when the girls and I are supposed to go shopping for our annual birthday bash. Hopefully I'll be able to get back late Friday night or at least by noon on Saturday.

On top of all of the drama at work, home life hasn't been any better. Tyrell's ass is definitely up to something. He had been coming home later and later each night and is always giving me a lame ass excuse. Another thing that lets me know that he's up to something is that he's been so overprotective of his phone lately. He used to leave his phone out and not even have a lock code on it, but now he takes that damn phone everywhere that he goes inside of the house. I woke up the other morning to go to the restroom, and saw him sitting in the living room. His eyes were glued to his phone, fingers just moving! He was reading and sending text messages at 1:00 in the damn morning! He was so engrossed with his phone that he didn't even notice me standing there.

I didn't say a word. I just crept out of the room, used the bathroom, and climbed back into bed. Of course once he heard the toilet flush, he came strolling through the bedroom door and got on his side of the bed, as if I didn't know that he was just making love to his damn phone. I'm sure he knew something was wrong because I turned my back to him, making sure that my ass was tucked securely under the covers. He got the hint because for the third consecutive night we slept back to back.

I look around my classroom once more to make sure that everything is in place. I'm even waiting on 5:00pm to go to Rico's; I'm heading there now! I know the other girls would be surprised that I would be the first one there.

Besides, if I get there early enough, I might be able to steal some time with Marcus. I haven't seen him in over a week, and I actually missed him. That's a scary thought to me, I reflect as I make my way to the parking lot. I'm still smiling when I make it to my car until I see a piece of paper sticking from under my windshield wiper.

Thinking it's just another flyer about a fundraiser or other event, I'm about to crumple it and throw it away, but a little voice tells me to look at it. What I see makes my blood boil. In scribbled red letters that are seemingly supposed to be blood, are the words, "Watch your back, bitch!"

Chapter Twenty-Six

Shaina

"Sometimes the truth might just come knocking on your door."

I can't remember a time when I have been both so excited and happy but also so nervous about the changes that are taking place in my life. I guess I would feel better if I could confide in my girls about everything, but I'm still trying to find the right moment to tell them what's going on with me. I mean, I know they're going to be pissed because we made a pact over the years to share everything with each other, no matter how bad, scandalous, or illegal it is. So not sharing my news with them is becoming harder each day, but all of that will change next week because I have decided that I'm going to share it all at our annual birthday party planning dinner next weekend. I will cross my fingers and hope that my girls understand, but after the interrogation that I got from Sheree last week about my dinner with Ahmad, I'm not so sure how they're going to handle it.

Even now just sitting here thinking about the fact that in a few months I will be debuting my first job as an event planner is just really unbelievable!! So much has happened in the year that I've been working hard on getting certified, and in the process of that I fell in love with a building that has become my dream event venue, Lyric's Loft.

"Mommy, mommy?" Lyric calls out to me as she runs into the room squealing with laughter.

"Hey Mommy's favorite girl. Let's go get lunch because Mommy is starving!" I take Lyric's hand and lead her downstairs to the kitchen.

While I prepare us a quick lunch of chicken salad, crackers, and fruit, I decide to call Morgan to check in with her. I haven't spoken with her much since she became an overnight mom. I'm curious to see how that's going, especially since for years Morgan has thrown herself into her career.

"Hey Mama Morgan," I joke when I hear her voice on the other end.

"Oh, so you've got jokes heifer? Girl you know I'm always hollering about having a baby, but damn. I didn't think my baby would come in the form of a teenager," she admits.

"I know that's right, but at least it's Niecey! She's such a sweetheart Morgan!"

"Yes, you're right. She is and honestly she doesn't seem to miss Tish at all. She seems so happy being in my home Shaina."

"Aww, that's great girl. I'm - " y words are interrupted by the ringing of the doorbell.

"Girl, hold on. I'm trying to figure out who in the heck is ringing my doorbell in the middle of the afternoon."

I opened the door to a young man looking as if standing on my porch in the middle of the day was the last place that he wanted to be.

"Are you Mrs. Xavier Ferber?" he asks in a squeaky little voice.

"Yes, I am." I answer, still unsure of who he is and why he's on my doorstep.

"You've been served. Have a nice day," he replies, shoving an envelope in my hand.

"What in the hell?" I can't believe my eyes as I stare at the envelope. I almost forgot that Morgan is on the phone until I hear her calling out my name.

"Shaina? Shaina? You're scaring me. Is everything okay?" her worry-filled voice snaps me back into reality.

"Girl, you are not going to believe this!! That was a court process server at the door. He just served me with court papers."

"What! That's crazy Shaina. You are the only one of us who doesn't even have a parking ticket," she says.

"I know Morgan. Stay on the line while I read out to you."

My hands are trembling, and my heart is racing as I prepare myself to read the document enclosed in the envelope. As I read the outside of the envelope, my fear and nervousness soon turn to confusion.

"Morgan, this is not addressed to me. It says Xavier's name on the envelope, not mine. Do you think I should open it?"

Morgan pauses before answering me. "If you don't open it, do you trust that Xavier is going to tell you what is going on with him that would lead to a process server being on your doorstep?"

She makes a good point. Xavier is not the most forthcoming when it comes to sharing important information with me, especially if it involves something that could potentially threaten our marriage. I open the document and read it.

"Oh my God, Morgan! It's from family court. Xavier has been ordered to show up for a paternity test for a child whose name is Xavier Ferber Jr.!!"

As I pause long enough to catch my breath, I vaguely hear Morgan telling me to not say anything to Xavier or anyone else. The last thing I hear her say is that she's on her way to me.

Chapter Twenty-Seven

Morgan

"There comes a point in most women's relationships when she has to pull the 'Freak Em Girl Dress' out of the closet."

I promise you, the shit that happens to my girls and me could very well be a made for TV movie. I can't think of a year since we've met that there hasn't been some type of drama in our lives.

Right now I'm sitting in the dining room of Shaina's well adorned home. She is upstairs getting dressed for us to go to Rico's, and I'm replaying in my mind the events of the past three hours.

About ten minutes after I arrived at Shaina's place, Xavier came walking quietly into the kitchen where we were sitting having a glass of Moscato. I could tell from the look on his face and his body language that he already knew about the impending paternity test. He took one look at the nearly empty bottle of wine on the countertop and the tears that were streaming down Shaina's face and immediately went on the defense.

"Look Shaina, it's no point in you crying and calling Morgan over here like it's such a damn big deal," he ranted, not even trying to console Shaina.

"Xavier, I just happened to be on the phone when she was served with the papers. So as the attorney for both of you and a best friend to both of you, there was no way that I was going to leave her here by herself to deal with this!" I told Xavier as he put his hands up in surrender.

"You're right, Morgan. I apologize. It's just that I had been trying so hard to keep this mess from going to court in the first place, which is why I hadn't told her yet."

He then got down on his knees and took Shaina's hands in his.

"Shaina, baby. Please believe me when I tell you that I will take care of this. I was already planning on calling Morgan today so that she could counsel me on what to do about this matter. Just trust me please baby."

It was at that moment that Shaina rose up like Sophia did in The Color Purple when she was about to punch the lights out of somebody. I stood as a wall of protection between the two of them because by the look of fury in Shaina's eyes and the balled up fists by her side, I didn't know what in the hell was about to happen.

"Trust you? Did you just say trust you Xavier Maurice Ferber? I will NEVER trust you again after this!! NEVER!!" Shaina spat at Xavier as she ran upstairs with Xavier close on her heels. I was about to leave until Xavier came back down to tell me that Shaina was getting dressed and that he would meet me at my office one day next week.

That was thirty minutes ago, and I'm really about to leave this time.

"Morgan. I'm ready," Shaina calls from the top of the stairs.

As I stood and gathered my things, I take a look up at Shaina, and all I can think is, *Oh damn*.

Shaina is wearing her "Freak Em Girl Dress"! It is a beautiful red dress with a V damn near all the way down to her belly button. Cleavage spills out of the top of her dress, and she clearly made sure her booty was looking delicious!! This is going to be one interesting night at Rico's.

Chapter Twenty-Eight

Maven

"It's good to have options instead of being an option."

"Hey Ahmad, I'll take a Ciroc with pineapple juice. And before you ask, Shaina should be here any minute now," I tell Ahmad as he smiles and then hurries away to place my drink order.

After the week I've had and that last conversation with Karver, I don't mind being the first one to arrive at Rico's tonight. I still can't believe that Karver confided in me about his desire to find his birth mother. I totally understand his situation because many of my siblings would probably never know our biological mom, which is probably why Karver and I hit it off better as friends than trying to be lovers.

The good thing is that now I have a new BFF who happens to be a man, which means maybe he can hook me up with one of his friends or relatives.

I smile as I see Ahmad walking back toward the table with my drink and a smirking Sheree clinging to his arm.

"Sheree, you'd better let go of Shaina's man before you catch a beatdown," I playfully jab at her.

"Well Shaina's not here yet, so I can play with her boy toy all I want," Sheree says as she sits down in the chair directly beside me.

"Hey girl, how's business going at the salon?" she asks me.

"Everything is good girl, and before you ask, no I'm not dating or screwing Karver or anyone else, but he did say that he might swing by tonight," I assure Sheree as I scan the room to make sure that I don't see him.

"That would be nice. Since you and Karver are best buds now, maybe one of his friends will be able to knock the cobwebs off of that coochie for you!!"

"Ha, ha Sheree," I laugh along with her, but she does have a point. It has been quite a while since I felt the touch of a man, and I can't say that I'm not in need right now.

"Maven, trust me, I do understand. The way Tyrell has been acting up lately, sex has been the last thing on my mind."

"Yeah, you can say that because you have the option to turn sex down, but unfortunately I don't have that choice."

"Well, maybe your options are about to expand," she says like she knows something I don't.

"What do you mean by that?" I ask. I follow Sheree's glance and look up to see Karver followed by a man. He waves at me and begina to walk toward the table. I subconsciously reach up to make sure my hair is straight and nervously pull on my skirt.

"Quit fiddling with yourself Maven. You look hot as usual. Now flash that gorgeous smile, stick out those nice breasts, and take another sip in case he is ugly as hell!" Sheree instructs with a laugh. I try not to burst out laughing as Karver and his friend stand before us.

"Hi boss lady. Hi Sheree. I'd like you to meet my friend, Houston," Karver says to us as I look up to get a better look at the handsome man standing beside him.

I can't believe my eyes! There, standing less than three feet away from me, is my middle school boyfriend, Houston Lewis!

"Hi Maven," he says with a smile. "Long time, no see."

Chapter Twenty-Nine

Maven

"It just may happen that someone from your past will walk into your present and help you build a better future."

I can't believe my eyes. I haven't seen Houston in over twenty years! His parents divorced when we were in the eighth grade, and the last I heard he had moved to New Orleans with his dad. Lawd, he was fine when we were kids, but now he's grown man fine.

"Hi, Houston, and yes it has been a long time. How have you been?"

"I've been decent. Ups and downs," he shrugs his broad shoulders. "Too much to talk about now. Maybe we can catch up over lunch or dinner one day this week," he asks.

"Sure, that will be great. Here's my business card. Just let me know when you are ready," I say as I smiled up at him and placed my business card in his hand.

Houston holds on to my hands for a few seconds, and I look down at our clasped hands, liking the way his chocolate skin looked next to mine. "Maven, I look forward to seeing you again. Ladies, enjoy your evening, and the next two rounds are on us."

"Now Maven, these are the kind of men that I like!" Sheree yells out.

"See you in the morning, Boss Lady," Karver says as he and Houston head toward the bar. I wait until I'm sure they are out of earshot before I turn to Sheree with a huge grin on my face.

"Oh my God, Sheree! When I last saw Houston he was standing in the parking lot with his dad telling me that he would come back for me one day. He gave me a little black box which contained a silver necklace with a cross pendant. We hugged, shared a quick kiss, and then he was gone."

"I remember that day because that's one of the few times that you didn't sit on the stoop braiding hair. You cried for days until you got that first phone call from Houston," Sheree remembers.

"Right. Once I knew that he was okay, it was back to the money and back to life of being the daughter of a crack addict."

"But Maven, remember that Houston said that one day he would come back for you. Maybe now that day has come."

"You're so right Sheree, but you know how I feel about relationships and men. I just don't want to open myself up, give so much of my heart to someone, and then get hurt or betrayed again," I admit.

"I know you don't, Maven. Hell, I don't trust men either, but you have to start somewhere. Besides Houston is someone who you've already loved once before. Maybe it's time that you take care of yourself and look out for your needs instead of focusing so much time and energy on the salon or locating your mom. Give Houston a chance, and see if he deserves to have a special place in your life," she advises.

"I guess. Hell, he can't be any worse than some of the other guys who I have let in my life that I know didn't deserve a place there."

Sheree and I both laugh as we reminisce about some of the clowns that I've gone on dates with or been in relationships with over the years.

"So, do I have your word that you're going to at least take Houston's call?" Sheree asks me.

"Yes, Sheree," I promised. "You have my word, and please promise me that you won't say anything to

Shaina or Morgan. I'm not ready to share my possible date with Houston just yet."

"Girl, you know I'll try, but you must remember that Morgan makes a living interrogating people; I'll do my best to keep this secret for you."

"Thanks Sheree; I'll drink to that."

As Sheree and I sip on our drinks, I give myself permission to steal a glance at Houston who is still standing at the bar talking to Karver and some other guys. Time has definitely been good to him. He still flashes that beautiful smile that I used to love when we were kids. He still has that curly hair that I loved playing in, and best of all he still has that walk that commands attention when he walks into the room.

I can see that he has put on some weight over the years, but so have I. In my mind that just means there's more to love. The more I look at him, the more I realize that I'm ready to have a man in my life. Don't get me wrong, I enjoy spending time with my girls, but there is only so much they could do for me.

At that very moment, as if he could feel my eyes on him, Houston turns around and our eyes lock. He flashes that beautiful smile, and I can feel my heart skip a beat. Not only that, I can also feel a warmth and tingling in my "special place" that I haven't felt in a long time. I can't believe that Houston is having this effect on me from across the room. I can only imagine what it will be like to feel his lips on my body, moving all the way from my neck to my-

I'm interrupted by Sheree nudging my shoulder and whispering, "Oh my damn!"

I looked up to see Morgan followed by Shaina. But this wasn't the usual Friday night, I have a husband and daughter at home Shaina. This was the Friday night, my husband has screwed up, I'm looking for a new love like Jody Watley, Shaina.

I don't know what is going on, but I can't wait to find out.

Chapter Thirty

Shaina

"Sometimes a woman has to do WHO or WHAT a woman has to do."

As I walk around the building that will soon be introduced to the world, or at least the city, as "Lyric's Loft," I can't help but smile when I think about Friday night at Rico's.

The one image I can't get out of my mind is the look on Maven and Sheree's faces when they saw me wearing my Freak Em Girl Dress. I don't think I had ever heard Sheree speechless before, but she just stood there and gaped at me for at least one whole minute before she finally responded.

"Damn Shaina! If I was still into girls, I would definitely take you home with me tonight. You are looking hot girl!! Which can only mean one thing. Xavier must have screwed up again!!"

Maven couldn't wait to chime in, agreeing with Sheree. "Yessss girl!! I can't wait to hear all of the juicy details. Let's call over your boyfriend, Ahmad, so that he can bring us our first round of drinks because I have a feeling that tonight is going to be one for the record books."

I only nodded my head as I took a seat, looked at my girls, and said, "Let the party begin!" With that I stood beside the table and started to bounce my ass to the rap song blasting from the speakers. Not wanting me to be the only one having a good time, the other girls all stood and begin bumping and grinding to the music.

The song finally stopped, and we all sat down just as Ahmad came over to the table. He was talking to the other girls and giving them their drinks, but his eyes were all over my body. My skin began to tingle, and my body begin to get hot all over.

By that time, our eyes locked. He leaned over and whispered in my ear, "Hi Shaina. You look amazing tonight. I've never seen you look so delicious, and I do mean that in every sense of the word."

I felt a wetness begin to pool in my center and my nipples hardened against my dress. I tried to steady my voice before I responded to him.

"Ahmad, thank you so much for our drinks. Here's a $100 bill. Keep them coming." I resisted the urge to smack Ahmad on his tight ass as he walked back to the bar.

I took a deep breath before I sat back at the table because I knew that three pairs of eyes would be on me, staring into my soul and waiting for answers since I'm sure they witnessed the sexual current that flowed between Ahmad and me.

"You are really living up to that freak em dress that you're wearing, Shaina," Sheree said. "You and Ahmad might as well have undressed each other and got it on right here on top of the table."

I smiled at Sheree. "Girl, as you know, I am a happily married woman. Ahmad and I are just really good friends."

"Girl, what the hell ever!" Sheree shouted over the music. "And we all know that whenever a woman wears a freak em dress it either means that her man is acting up, or she's trying to see if she still has it."

"And in your case," Morgan added, "It's both."

It was at that moment that I decided to share with Maven and Sheree the events from earlier with Xavier and the paternity test issue.

As I expected, Maven told me to wait until the court date before I made a final decision, and of course Sheree told me to leave Xavier and give Ahmad a ride, literally.

Their two differing opinions were both true to how I felt about my marriage right now. But I refused to let my mess of a marriage deter me from my goal of making Lyric's Loft the most popular entertainment venue this city will ever see!

So now almost a week later, I still smile when I think of the look on Ahmad's face when he saw me wearing that sexy dress.

The look he gave me was the look that Xavier used to give me when we were first married. I don't think he's looked at me like that in months because he's been too busy keeping secrets. Well, this time I have kept a secret too. He has no idea that I am a licensed event planner or even that I've purchased Lyric's Loft. But he'll find out soon enough. Our annual birthday party was only six weeks away, so I had to make sure that this night was perfect.

"Look here trick, you need to get your head out of the clouds. We have work to do," a voice jars me out of my thoughts. I turn around and smile at the intruder.

"Hi, Christopher. Thanks for helping me out with ordering the furniture. I've always enjoyed your funky sense of style, so I knew you'd be the perfect one to help me. Plus you're cheap!!"

"Okay hussy, don't get it twisted. I'm only cheap for you because you're a friend," Christopher cracks back at me.

"Yeah, yeah. Now where is this amazingly, sexy, talented bartender that I'm supposed to meet?"

"Here I am," calls a familiar voice from the entrance of the building. I instantly recognize it.

"Ahmad? What are you doing here?"

Chapter Thirty-One

Morgan

"Mixing business with friends usually leaves a bad taste in your mouth."

"MariCruz, let me know when Mr. Ferber gets here. I need to meet with him before we go to meet the judge."

"Yes ma'am, chica."

I can't wait to get to the judge's chambers today. This child paternity suit with Xavier and one of his lovers has been a thorn in my side for the past two weeks. Every time I get a court date set, the child's grandmother has ninety thousand two hundred twenty-two excuses. Once the child was too sick to travel the 30 miles to get him to the clinic for the blood test, but that didn't stop her from trying to file for child support payments even though Xavier hasn't officially been ruled to be the father.

I finally convinced a judge to compel the grandmother to bring the child in last week for a mandatory paternity test. This only came after the grandmother was threatened to be jailed for being in contempt of court.

So today we're all meeting in Judge Hawthorne's chambers to find out the results of the DNA test. Although we all warned Shaina about Xavier, I'm still hoping and praying that this child is not Xavier's. Shaina has been through so much during her marriage to Xavier, and I just don't know if she could take anything else.

"Ms. Morgan," MariCruz's voice calls through on my intercom, "Mr. Ferber is here to see you."

"Thanks MariCruz. Please send him in." I watch as Xavier walks in looking very confident.

"Hey Morgan, I must say once again thank you for helping me in this matter. I know this is hard for you because Shania is one of your best friends," Xavier says as he gives me a brief hug.

"Yes, I must admit that it is a little awkward, but I don't mind because I love both of you. Have you not forgotten that you were actually my boyfriend first?" I joke as Xavier and I prepare to walk the short distance to the courthouse.

"How could I forget Morgan? If it wasn't for you I would have been beaten up on my first day of first grade!" We both laugh as we discuss how I had saved

Xavier from a beating when he accidentally stepped on the shoe of Terry Jenkins, the school bully and my cousin.

"Yes, I was literally standing there in tears when you came up, punched him in the gut, and then yelled at him, "Terry! Leave that boy alone! I can't wait to get home and tell Daddy!"

I laugh loudly as I remember that from that day on Xavier, Terry, and I became inseparable. We were all best friends and had remained that way for years until Xavier and I met Shaina. Shaina was in love with Xavier as soon as she saw those damn green eyes, but I couldn't blame her. I had once fallen in love with them too, but he always saw me as his little sister, which was fine because once I met Shaina I knew that she would become like a sister to me too.

"Yes Xavier, those were the good old days, and you know since you and Shaina first got together, I've tried to stay neutral and not take sides. But you're going to have to come clean to Shaina if you ever want to get your marriage back on track again. I don't know how much of your bull that Shaina is going to continue to take from you," I tell Xavier in a serious tone.

"I know, I know Morgan. I'm going to do that as soon as all of this crap is over. You have my word."

"Okay. Now remember what I said. Let me do most of the talking. This judge and I have been in the courtroom before, and she is usually pretty fair, but please don't try to run that pretty boy, green-eyed game on her like you do with other women. She'll hold you in contempt and throw your ass in jail if you even think about it!" I warn Xavier as we step onto the elevator.

"Yes ma'am, I got you Morgan. You lead. I'll follow. Just like old times," he says with a smile.

"Okay, let's do this. We step off the elevator and walk down the hall to the judges' chambers. I say a quick prayer before we walk into the room. Not only will the outcome of this paternity test affect my reputation, since I had put myself at risk by asking the judge for a favor and practically promising the judge that the grandmother was just after Xavier's money, but more importantly it will affect the marriage of two of my best friends.

Two hours later Xavier and I emerge from the courtroom ecstatic with cries of victory. The child in question was found to have zero percent chance of having any relations to Xavier. We also found out the grandmother knew this all along; she was actually hoping that Xavier wouldn't fight it and try to settle out of court so as not to ruin his business, his marriage, or his reputation.

Xavier actually picks me up and swung me around.

"Thank you so much Morgan!" he yells excitedly.

"You're welcome Xavier. Now put me down please."

"Oh yeah. I'm sorry" Xavier says as he places me back on the ground. "I'm just so glad that this whole damn mess is finally over! Now maybe Shaina and I can begin repairing our marriage."

"Yes Xavier, I really hope so for your sake, but most importantly for my god-daughter. She deserves to be raised by both of her parents, just like we were."

"You're right, Morgan. Now you must let me treat you to an early dinner to repay you."

"No, no Xavier. You don't have to do that," I appreciate his offer but I really just want him to get back to Shaina and tell her the news.

"I know I don't have to do it Morgan. I want to do it. Besides you need to help me think of what to buy Shaina for her birthday this year. The big party is only about eight weeks away, and I have no idea what to get her this year."

"Well . . . I guess we might as well get that part over with now. Let me get my car, and I'll follow you there."

"We can just ride together, and I'll bring you back to get your car. I have to drive right back past here to go home," he tells me.

"Cool. Well, since you're paying, I want to go to the most expensive place in the whole damn city!" I joke with Xavier.

"No problem. McDonald's it is," he shoots back.

"You're not getting off that easy man."

Chapter Thirty-Two

Sheree

"If you go searching for something, chances are you'll find it."

I definitely enjoyed my time in ATL. It's always good to get away from home and my students. And of course Tyrell. When he found out that I would be gone for three days, he started acting like he was going to miss me so much. Like that episode of Martin when Gina is going on a business trip, and Martin starts whining and looking out the window and shit. That's how Tyrell's ass was acting. He kept hugging on me, kissing me, and telling me that he didn't know what he was going to do without me for a whole three days.

Yeah right. Now I know that was a lie because this is my last day on my trip, and I've only talked to him maybe two or three times in the entire three days that I've been here.

When I asked him about it of course he accused me of just trying to check on him to make sure that he's not doing anything wrong. When I responded by pointing out that I have only talked to him a few times since I've been gone, his reply was "Damn Sheree. You act like you've been gone for a month. You ain't been gone but three damn days!"

I had to hold the phone away and stare at it to make sure that bastard was talking to me like that. If it wasn't for the fact that I was sitting at lunch with a group of teacher friends, I would've cussed his ass out and told him to get his shit and get out of my house. But I remained as calm as I could and just told him that I had to go back in a meeting.

That was yesterday, and I hadn't actually spoken to Tyrell since then. He sent me plenty of text messages trying to apologize for what he had said. I only responded once with a simple, "Okay."

What Tyrell doesn't know is that I am already on to him. While I was gone, I had a feeling in my gut that he was back to his old cheating ways again. So I did what any woman would or should do; I became a chocolate detective. Tyrell and I have been together for so long that I know him pretty well, so I know that he still has the same password for his email that he had when I first met him more than three years ago.

Now, although I've never been the kind of woman to check up on my man, go through his phone, or follow him, I feel that Tyrell has left me with no other choice. I know in my heart that it's time to move on, but I really want to find some evidence so that his ass can't put those googly eyes on me, get my panties wet, and screw his way back into my life like he's done so many times before. I can't let that happen this time, which is why I decided to work on my plan while I was in Atlanta, and as I the old saying goes, "If you go out looking for something, you're going to find it." And boy did I find it!!

When I went through Tyrell's emails, at first I didn't see anything but a bunch of junk emails, and I felt like an ass for even going through his shit in the first place. However, something told me to click on that Social tab. I did, and that's when all of the shit that Tyrell had been up to punched me in my stomach. This negro has been on several dating sites. Even as I was going through all of this, I knew that this could only be the tip of the iceberg, so I decided to go to one of his profiles to see what he's been really up to. There his ass was, smiling on his picture like he didn't have a care in the world and not only that, his profile said that he was married. He even had the nerves to be wearing a wedding band!

At first I couldn't understand why he would lie and say he was married, but then I realized that this probably earned him more attention from other women who were themselves married and didn't want the baggage that comes along with a single man. Also some women don't give a damn these days about a man having a girlfriend or a wife (hell I have knowingly been the "other woman" before), so it's not surprising that he would lie about being married.

To say I'm not hurt by what I saw would be a lie because I am hurt, but most importantly I'm pissed because I feel that I've wasted time being in a relationship that has only been sexually fulfilling. Nothing about our relationship has fulfilled my heart or my soul, and I feel like Tyrell being in my life has hindered me from moving forward with other passions in my life, like my writing. I started a novel a few years before meeting Tyrell, but I haven't written a single word since then.

So now I have the ammunition that I need to finally remove Tyrell from my life once and for all. It couldn't have come at a better time. Our annual birthday party was coming up soon, and for the first time in three years I will be attending as a single woman, without Tyrell following me around the whole night or acting jealous when he sees a man give me a hug.

As I think about the Tyrell's, I can't help but think back to that note that was left on my car a few weeks ago. I'm beginning to think that maybe one of Tyrell's bitches got bold enough to try to scare me into leaving him. I mean, I did notice that he's been messaging one particular woman several times a day, and I can tell from their messages that they've met in person and have already had sex multiple times.

I actually don't blame him because she's a beautiful Latina with a nice ass like mine, so I understand why he's so attractive to her. That just goes to show that no matter how good you are to a man, how great your sex is, or how big your ass, is if a man wants to cheat there's nothing you can do about it.

Now, as I sit in this taxi about five minutes from my house, I mentally prepare myself for the moment when I tell Tyrell that it's over. I'm glad that I'm getting home a few hours earlier than Tyrell expected me to because he should be at work for a few more hours, and I will have time to pack up his few belongings and have a drink before I have to confront him.

As we pull up to my driveway, I'm a little confused when I see my truck parked in the front of the house. I know that Tyrell should still be at work. Hell, it's only 1:00, and he has to work until 5:00 or 6:00 this evening. As I wait for the driver to retrieve my luggage from the trunk, I can't help but feel a sensation of dread taking over my body.

"Thanks," I say to the driver as he places my luggage on the front steps. I gently insert my key in to unlock the door, and then I decide to step out of my heels. I'm trying to be as quiet as I can be so I won't alert Tyrell that I'm in the house. As I make my way towards the back of the house, my heart begins to feel as if it's going to beat out of my chest.

The closer to the bedroom door I get, the more I'm clear that there is no mistake that Tyrell is at home. In our bedroom. Screwing the hell out of another woman. In my bed.

I stand at the bedroom door and attempt to gather myself before flinging it open.

Tyrell is in the throes of passion as a woman rides him like a champ. I don't think. I just react.

I charge forward, knocking her ass to the ground before I begin to attack Tyrell with my fists, cursing and screaming at him. He tries to deflect my blows while I continue to go at him until that bitch decides to jump in. At that moment, I turn my attention to her. It seems like hours that I'm kicking her ass before I feel a pain that starts in my arm, and then moves toward my chest. I clutch my chest in pain, and then everything around me goes black.

Chapter Thirty-Three

Sheree

"Although you never think of ending it all, you do wish that it all would end."

As I sit in my bed watching television, I can't help but think about the past week of my life. Not only did I walk into MY home, that I pay the mortgage on every month, and catch that bastard Tyrell screwing another woman, but I had also suffered a major anxiety attack that had landed me in the emergency room. I was admitted into the hospital and had to spend two nights there under observation. The physician warned me that if I didn't get the stress in my life under control, the next time it could be a heart attack instead of a case of anxiety.

I know he's right. Between my job and Tyrell, my life has become quite stressful over the past few years, and I surely don't want to end up on heart medication or worse than that. I don't want to let Tyrell's ass be the cause of me having a damn heart attack. I can't let anyone or anything have that much power over my life anymore.

Since I've been old enough to know what pain, betrayal, and abandonment are, there hasn't been a year in my life that I haven't experienced one of those negative emotions. Now mind you, I don't walk around crying "Woe is me" all the time, but there are times in my life that I just wonder if things will ever get better. When do I have to stop getting my heart broken? When will I ever feel that I'm doing enough in my life? Would I ever get over not growing up with my father?

I was abandoned by my father when I was only one year old. My mom was only sixteen when she got pregnant with me, and my dad promised her that he would stand by her and help to take care of me, but he bounced soon after I celebrated my first birthday, vowing to my mom that he would come back for us. Almost 40 years later, and he still hadn't honored his word. I have only seen him five times in my whole life.

I know I'm one of many women suffering from "daddy issues" because of my pretty much non-existent relationship with my dad, or sperm donor, as I often refer to him. My issues with betrayal and abandonment are deeply rooted, which is why I seem to attract needy men. I feel that if a man needs me, then maybe he won't leave me like my dad did.

However, my dad doesn't hold the title of being the only grown-up who has ever betrayed me or caused me pain. My mom's betrayal has caused me to keep a family secret that not even any of the girls know about. It is one that haunts me every day, and I often ask God why did he choose me to carry such a burden? I know that my heart has been heavy for years, which is one of the reasons that I'm always surrounding myself with men and a great time.

More than twenty years ago when I was fifteen years old, I thought I had met the love of my life. His name was Lewis James Johnson, but everyone called him LJ. His parents were divorced, and he had moved with his dad to my housing projects in the summer of my 9th grade year. Right away I was attracted to Lewis, not because of his smooth dark chocolate skin, his wavy black hair, or his beautiful smile. It was because he was the best damn Uno, Spades, and Dominoes player that I had ever met! Besides my grandfather and uncle of course.

Once LJ realized that I could play as well as or better than him, we became fast best friends. With him not having a mom in his life, and my dad being MIA, we shared a bond that was just as tight and sometimes closer than the bond that I shared with my girls. He spent many days at my apartment, and I at his. We had become a part of each other's dysfunctional families, and our parents trusted us around each other because most people just saw us as having a brother/sister type of relationship.

Well, one day when our parents left us alone in the apartment, we decided to share our first kiss. It was one that I still remember after all of these years have passed. Lewis grabbed my chin, looked into my eyes, and gently kissed my lips. My body reacted in a way that I had never felt before.

A heat began to move from my lips all the way to my core, and in my panties a pool of wetness formed. Since none of those feelings were familiar to me before the kiss that I shared with LJ, I didn't know what to do. So I just let him kiss me again and stood there with a goofy smile on my face.

I fell head over heels in love with LJ at that moment, and from that day on we became teenaged lovers. We already spent all of our free time together, so the only thing that really changed was that he called me his girlfriend when we were away from our parents. He even let me wear his gold rope chain and his Varsity football jacket to school every day.

Everything was all good until that one night when LJ and I were left alone once again. Our parents had gone into town to play bingo as they did on most nights. Although LJ and I tried really hard to just kiss and touch each other's bodies, apparently it wasn't enough to satisfy us. Before I knew it, he was pulling down my pants and entering me.

The pain was almost unbearable, but LJ made me feel so beautiful and loved that I soon begin to enjoy it. For once in my life, I could experience an unconditional love from someone who told me that he would protect me and love me forever.

I believed LJ when he told me that, and after our night of unexpected, awkward but tender love-making, we both decided that we would keep our bodies from each other until we graduated high-school and could ask for our parents for permission to marry.

Everything was going according to our plan until about eight weeks after that night when I begin to feel sick. I was vomiting every day, and I couldn't keep anything in my stomach. At first, I thought it was just a virus, but when I told my mom, she asked, "When was the last time I bought you some sanitary napkins." When I couldn't remember, she lunged at me and yelled, "I know you're pregnant whore! You've made a mistake, but I'm not gonna let you embarrass this family!"

As I sat there and cried, I thought of what LJ would say when I told him. As if she could read my mind, my mom told me that I'd better not even think about letting LJ or anyone else know that I was about to become a mother in the next seven months.

At that time, I didn't know what my mom had planned, or how she thought I would be able to keep the pregnancy a secret after I started to show. I soon found out. The very next month my mother packed up my siblings and me and moved us to New Orleans. We stayed there for a little over a year. Long enough for me to give birth to my daughter and long enough for my mom to tell everyone back home that while we were gone there had been a new addition to the family. My mom told them that SHE had given birth to a beautiful baby girl, Zoe Latrece.

I couldn't believe that my mom had decided to take my daughter away from me and claim her as her own! But what was I to do? I was fifteen years old with no home of my own and no means to take care of a child. Plus my mom threatened me that if I ever told anyone the truth, she would take Zoe, and I would never see either of them again. Although I didn't know if my mom was for real, I had learned over the years not to cross her. So as much as it hurt me to live with Zoe and not be able to raise her as my own, that's what I had to do.

Over the years, everyone always remarked how much Zoe and I looked alike. I would just tell them that we looked so much alike because we both looked like our mom. Whenever Zoe questioned about her dad, I would just say that he was a very handsome and nice man and that Mom had never told him that he had a daughter.

Now after over two decades, life had come full-circle because I had seen on Facebook that LJ was back in town. Maybe this was a sign that it was time to tell Zoe Latrece the truth. That her big sister was in fact her mother.

Chapter Thirty-Four

Maven

"You can't take an old attitude into a new situation and expect to see a different outcome."

To say that my date with Houston was good or even great would be a huge understatement! The date was amazing!!! In fact, it was hands down the best date I have ever been on.

Houston is just as sweet as I remember him being when we were in middle school. He is just very thoughtful, and I was reminded of that on our date in many ways. He made sure that he was a complete gentleman the entire night, pulling out my chair for me at the restaurant, praying over our meal before we ate, and being very attentive during the date. His eyes never left my eyes, and he listened intently as I tried to cram as much of our over twenty year separation into one night of dinner, drinks, and desserts as I could. When the night ended, Houston walked me to my car, and we shared a very intimate kiss.

Since then we have pretty much been inseparable. He came to the shop at least three times in the last week just to bring me lunch or take me out to dinner. The shop has been buzzing with news and gossip about my new "boo-thang" as Ms. Clarice calls him.

I must admit that it does felt really good to have someone who takes care of me for a change. Houston believed in pampering me and spoiling me, and he had no problems telling everyone around us that I was HIS woman. He was always telling me how much he couldn't wait for us to take our relationship to the next level.

Although I didn't ask him, I often wondered what he meant by "the next level". I mean don't get me wrong; I was enjoying every moment that I spent with Houston, but I was also very protective of my heart. It had been broken too many times by too many people, and for years I had placed a wall around my heart that no one had been able to penetrate.

We had just sort of fallen into a routine already. I would go to his place after work, or when I left early he would come to my apartment.

Houston and I got along so perfectly that it was scary. I mean I haven't let anyone into my life, my heart, or my bed since my ex, and that was more than nine months ago. My ex had truly betrayed me, and it hurt so bad that I promised myself I would take a break from men for a while.

No, that didn't mean that I was going to switch teams and start dating women; not that I didn't think about it, but that's just not me. I just made up my mind that I was going to take the time to date myself and get to know me all over again.

For years I have gone from one relationship or hookup to the next, not giving myself time to breathe or even figure out what happened to make things go to the left. In the midst of this, I feel like I lost a little sense of who I am. I was so busy trying to please the penis in my life at the time that I often put myself and what was important to me on the back burner.

Consequently my ex, Kaleel, took full advantage of the fact that I was always falling prey to someone who could sense my weaknesses and my vulnerabilities. It's like he had some type of "woman who is in desperate need of a man" magnet that drew me right to him. Kaleel wined, dined, and sexed me down at the beginning of our relationship.

And of course I was so happy to have someone that paid me that much attention that I ignored the red flags that were knocking me upside my head. Soon enough, Kaleel was knocking me down with his hurtful, mean words and his hands. This was one of the darkest times in my life because I had always strived to prove myself to be a boss in every sense of the word. Hell, I had been taking care of myself and my siblings since I was just thirteen years old. I had been an entrepreneur and a business owner for over sixteen years, and I yet I couldn't stand up to Kaleel. I was so embarrassed that I couldn't even talk to the other girls about what was going on behind closed doors.

So I just put on a fake smile, covered my bruises with different hairstyles and Mac foundation and concealer, and pretended like everything was all good in my world. I was Kaleel's personal punching bag for more than six months before I made up my mind that I was done. Well, actually God made up my mind for me.

I was at the shop one night. It was just Cash and me, and we were working late to finish up with inventory when one of my long time clients came running up to the front door of the salon. She was banging on the glass door and screaming at the top of her lungs, "Help! Someone help me please!" Cash hurried to unlock the door, and it took me a while to recognize her. Her face was covered with blood, her right eye was swollen shut, and bruises traveled from her neck to every place that my eyes scanned on her body.

As Cash ran to call 911, I sat her down to find out who in the hell had done this to her. Her answer shouldn't have shocked me, but it did. Her husband and the father of her four kids had severely beat her on this day, which was one day before they were set to leave for a cruise to celebrate their ten year wedding anniversary. All because she didn't want to wear the dress that he had chosen for her to wear during their vow renewal ceremony.

As I sat there and waited on the police and the ambulance to get there, I promised myself that I would leave Kaleel that night, and I did. Surprisingly, after two weeks of trying to apologize and beg me to come back, he suddenly left me alone. Last I heard, he had moved in with another woman.

Now sitting here at my desk and thinking back to that time, I realize that I am blessed that I got out of that situation with Kaleel sooner rather than later and that I'm blessed to have Houston back in my life. However, I must admit that my past relationships have left me jaded. I keep waiting on the shoe to drop, for something to go wrong.

I mean, I know that Houston is not perfect, no one is, but he just seems too good to be true.

My cell phone ringing pulled me from my thoughts. I see that it's Karver and I pick up immediately.

"Hey Karver. Are you enjoying your day off?" I joke because I know that Karver is stuck at the DMV today, and everybody knows how easily that can turn into an all-day affair.

"Very funny boss lady," he chuckles. "I'm actually just leaving. I'm finally able to say that I'm a registered and licensed driver again."

"Well, I'm happy for you. Plus I'm looking forward to you going to run all of my errands for me."

Karver laughs before responding, "Even though you know I don't mind doing anything for you, it seems as if my man, Houston, has got you covered."

"Ooh. Mr. Messy. I guess you're right," I tell him.

"I know I'm right Maven. He's a good guy, and you're a good woman so that makes the two of you great together. Houston is like my brother, and you're like my sister, so I'm happy for both of you."

"Thanks Karver! You're right. I just need to sit back and enjoy."

"That's my girl. Now, I have a serious matter that I want to discuss with you."

"Yes Karver," I nervously ask. "What's going on now?"

"Well, remember that I hired that private investigator to help me locate my birth mother?"

"Yes, does he have any news? I ask.

"The P.I. just told me that he had some pertinent information. The bad news is that he hasn't located my birth mother yet. The good news is that he thinks he has located one of her other children," Karver explains.

"That's awesome Karver. So what's the next step?"

"I'm going to meet up with him next Friday.

That's the night before our annual birthday bash, so maybe you'll have something to celebrate too!" I excitedly tell Karver.

"I hope so Maven. I really do."

"Just have faith Karver, and claim it. Speak it into existence. Either way it goes, you're my family now, and I'll be there to support you."

Chapter Thirty-Five

Morgan

"The mind and the body are often not on the same page."

For the first time in years, I have to admit that I'm not looking forward to our annual birthday bash, which is a little over four weeks away. How can I be when my life is practically falling apart around me? How can I stand in front of all of my friends, family, and colleagues and pretend to be in a celebratory mood when I don't feel an ounce of celebration in my life? How am I going to be able to look at my girls knowing that I'm keeping a secret from them that will rip our more than thirty years of friendship apart in a way that will be irreparable?

I don't think that any of them will understand what I'm going through or even how I could allow myself to get caught up in such a scandalous situation. Many times over the past week I've thought of calling Sheree or Maven to get their advice, but right now just isn't the right time to put my burdens on them.

Sheree is still recovering from her hospitalization over that foolishness with Tyrell, and Maven, for once, has found a man who takes her away from the salon and her screwed up family life. Last time I talked with her, she was still trying to track down her mom. I definitely can't and won't bother her with my issues.

And Shaina. Well there's no way in hell that I can talk to her about my problem. I mean, how was I supposed to tell Shaina that I, one of her best friends for more than thirty years, the one who practically introduced her to Xavier, the friend who had held her and consoled her after Xavier had cheated on her for the first time, the friend who had just represented her husband in the child paternity suit and child support case, had actually slept with her husband??!!!

Even now just thinking about it has me sitting in my office at my desk with my head in my hands. I never thought in a million years that I would be involved in an adulterous affair, let alone one that involved one of my best friends and her husband, a man who has always been like a brother to me. I mean yes, Xavier is a very handsome and sexy man, but I don't look at him in that way, so I'm shocked that we ended up in bed together in the first place.

It all happened so fast that I've been having trouble putting together what led to Xavier and me waking up in each other's arms. I remember Xavier asking to take me out to dinner after we left the courthouse following his paternity suit, which we won. Of course I didn't think anything was wrong with that since Xavier and I have been friends forever, and he did assure me that Shaina would try to join us later.

Xavier took me to one of my favorite seafood restaurants because he knows how much I love seafood, especially crab legs. We had such a good time at dinner, and I enjoyed having a male's perspective on dating. He even listened to me gripe about my issues with Tish and how Niecey had really embraced her new life of living with me.

Xavier also confided in me about his role in the issues that he and Shaina were experiencing in their marriage. He told me how Shaina had become really distant and secretive, and that he sometimes wondered if she was having an affair. Although I hated to take Xavier's side, the other girls and I had already discussed the fact that Shaina had been a little closed lipped lately. Whenever we mentioned it to her, Shaina just promised us that she would reveal everything to us the night of the party, so we just dropped the issue.

Since Xavier and I have been friends forever, I feel really comfortable with him, and I let my guard down and had more than the two drink maximum that I allot myself. When Xavier saw that I was a little bit tipsy, he offered to drive me home. I tried to get him to just call me a taxi or call one of the other girls to come take me home, but he reminded me that we were friends and that friends are supposed to look out for each other.

I agreed because even though I'm an attorney, I know that there is no use in arguing with Xavier. Besides he did have a point, especially when it was very obvious that I didn't need to drive anywhere that night, and there had been many times that Xavier, Tyrell, and any of the other boyfriends or hookups of the group had been our designated drivers over the years.

On the ride to my place, Xavier and I talked and laughed as we reminisced on many of the crazy times we'd shared in our childhood. It did feel good to not worry about anything else and be free to think about myself, if only for a moment.

By the time we pulled into my garage, I was thankful that Xavier had driven me home because I was so tired, and all I wanted to do was crawl into my bed and go to sleep. Xavier helped me up the stairs to my bedroom as I stumbled and held onto him to battle the spinning that was starting to build up in my head. I finally made it to my bedroom and collapsed onto my bed. Xavier left out telling me that he was going downstairs to fix me a hangover concoction and get me some aspirin. I could only mumble a reply because I was already feeling all warm and fuzzy inside, and I was ready for a night of deep sleep.

The next thing I remember was being in the middle of one of the most sensual dreams that I had ever experienced in my life. I was laying in my bed and a very handsome stranger was pleasing me with his mouth, licking and kissing my swollen clit as he made me cream all over his tongue. I grabbed his head and pulled him close into my folds as he continued his assault on my clit until I was literally crying real tears. He then cupped his hands under my butt and teased me with his fingers. My womanhood gripped his fingers, and I could hear him groaning when he realized how tight she was. He soon replaced his fingers with his swollen manhood and began to tease my opening with his hard tip. I could feel a tingling sensation begin to fill up in my belly as he slowly glided, inch by inch, his lengthy hardness into my wet opening. As he finally filled me up, he began to thrust deeper and deeper, stopping only to kiss me on my breasts.

It was this moment that I realized that this dream was seeming too real. I opened my eyes, and it hit me that this was no dream, and this was not a stranger. He was Xavier, one of my best friends, and the husband of one of my other best friends. I tried to push Xavier off, but even though my mind was telling me, "Hell no!" my body was enjoying it too much.

It had been so long since I had a man inside of me, and even longer since I had been taken to this height of ecstasy. I slowly gave in to the pleasure, and I let myself enjoy all that Xavier was giving me. He made love to me in a way that drove me to call out his name over and over again.

When it was over, Xavier just pulled me into his arms, held me close, and whispered in my ears, "I'm so sorry Morgan." I could feel the tears streaming down my face as I was torn between feelings of deep betrayal towards my friend and feelings of sexual satisfaction.

Chapter Thirty-Six

Morgan

"Your body will betray you if you're not careful."

I was interrupted from my memories when the door to my office was flung open and in marched Xavier with MariCruz chasing him.

"I'm so sorry Ms. Morgan. I tried to stop Mr. Ferber from barging in here, but he wouldn't listen to me" explains an exasperated looking MariCruz.

"It's no problem MariCruz. Please give Mr. Ferber and me some privacy, and hold all of my calls," I tell her.

"Yes ma'am," she answers as she leaves my office, but not before giving Xavier a look that shows her disdain and disapproval of his behavior.

"Xavier, what in the hell is wrong with you busting into my office like this??!!" I yell at him.

"Morgan you can't keep avoiding me. We have to discuss what happened with us," he shouts back at me.

"No, Xavier, we don't. What happened between us was a huge mistake that should have never happened and that won't happen again. Ever. How am I supposed to look at Shaina knowing that not only did I screw her husband, but that I also enjoyed it??" I clasp my hand over my mouth and turn my back to Xavier as I realize that I just admitted to Xavier that I actually enjoyed our night of passion.

Xavier voice calms, "Damn Morgan. I thought it was just me. I know that I sort of took advantage of the situation, but I promise you that I didn't plan this. When I came upstairs to bring you some medicine, I couldn't help but notice how beautiful and peaceful you looked while you were sleeping. I just sat there on your bed and stared at you for what seemed like forever. I know I should've left Morgan, but something kept drawing me to stay there. And then when you stirred in your sleep, your dress inched up just a little bit. Enough for me to see your luscious thighs -"

"Please stop Xavier! Stop!" I plead. I can't believe we're even talking about this.

"Morgan, just listen to me. I sat there and watched you, and I saw the sexy black panties that were covering your triangle, and I couldn't help myself. I took my fingers and gently pulled your panties to the side. You were so wet and warm that I just had to have a taste, so then I buried my face between your thighs and just inhaled your sweetness until my tongue begin to move on its own."

I just stand there because I'm afraid that if I say anything, Xavier will hear the lust in my voice.

"Morgan, please say something. I know that you didn't plan on this happening. Neither did I, but now we must figure out what's next for us," Xavier says to me as I continue to keep my back to him.

"What's next for you Xavier is leaving my office and pretending like that night two weeks ago never happened. What's next for me is taking all of the phone calls that I've missed while meeting with you, and what's next for us is showing up to the annual birthday party in a little over a month and having a great time as friends. Nothing more. Nothing less."

Xavier walks across the room until he is standing right behind me. He leans in so close that I can feel the hairs on the back of my neck begin to stand up.

"Okay, Morgan. I'm going to leave you alone for now, but trust me we are going to have to revisit this issue again. I know I'm not the only one who felt the powerful connection that we shared when I was buried deep inside of you. So you can continue to fight this, but I'll be ready when you want it again," Xavier says and I can feel the heat from his breath on my neck. He moves the hair away from my face and gently kisses my neck.

As much as I want to protest and ignore his kisses, my body betrays me, and I can soon feel a pool of wetness forming in my panties.

It wasn't until I heard Xavier's footsteps and the door shut behind him that I allowed myself to breathe.

I have six weeks to get myself prepared for this party and seeing Xavier and Shaina together again for the first time since that night.

Chapter Thirty-Seven

Shaina

**"Easy decisions are not always good, and good
decisions are not always easy."**

I am one tired sister. I'm so glad that Lyric spent
the night with her grandmother because there is no way
that I can get up with her this morning. Besides, it's
customary that after our epic party we go to brunch at
our favorite spot, Rico's. However, after all of the
fireworks from last night, I didn't know if the girls will
be up for still seeing each other today. I'm sure that at
this moment, they are just like me. Still half-clothed,
lying in bed trying to figure out the next move.

That's exactly what I'm doing right now. Staring
at the walls of my soon to be former bedroom. Relishing
in the fact that last night's party was just the beginning
of the next chapter in my book of life.

As I reflect on last night's party, I think about
the moment that I had by myself in "Lyric's Loft". I
arrived there early to make sure that things were going
to run smoothly with the setup for the party because it

was so important and so personal to me on so many levels.

Yes, it was our annual birthday celebration, but this was unlike any other birthday party that we've had over the years. This year I was taking my first steps towards establishing my own brand that would not be attached to my family or my husband. Lyric's Loft was my baby, and I had labored long and hard to bring this vision to life. For the first time in a long time, I had accomplished something that I was proud of and that I could share with all of my family and friends. As hard as it was to keep the secret from anyone, in the end I'm glad that I did it on my own. It gives me such a sense of pride.

So standing in the open foyer of the building was truly a surreal moment for me. As I looked around the spacious room at the décor, the walls draped in black fabric, the black linoleum dance floor engraved with all of our initials, the tables covered with black linen, the chairs with different colored sashes, and the bars equipped with the most exquisite liquors that money could buy, I could feel a wave of emotion beginning to overtake me. It was a mixture of excitement, nervousness, confidence, and total giddiness about the festivities that would begin in the next hour. As I wiped away the tears that had begun to fall from my eyes, I felt that Ahmad was standing behind me.

I didn't have to turn around to know that he was there. I could smell the fragrance of his cologne, a delicious blend of citrus and wood entangled with his own masculine scent. Just knowing he was in such close proximity to me caused my body to react in a way that I couldn't hide if I tried. I worked hard to control my breathing as I turned around to face Ahmad.

"Hi Ahmad. I'm so glad that you're here to help me. I can't thank you enough. You're a life saver. You can go ahead and start setting up. Guests should be arriving soon, and-"

"Shaina. Slow down," Ahmad interrupted me as he put his hands on my shoulders and gazed lovingly into my eyes. I just need you to take a deep breath. I wanted to get here a few minutes earlier because I was hoping to catch you by yourself," he admitted.

"Why is that Ahmad? Why did you want to have some private time with me?" I asked even though my heart was beating faster and faster and my nipples were tingling with anticipation.

"Because I wanted to do this," he whispered and then leaned down, grabbed my face with his hands, and planted the sweetest, most delicate kiss that my lips had ever had the pleasure of receiving. I was utterly speechless for a few moments, so I just stood there, imagining how his lips would feel on other parts of my body.

"Shania, I hope I didn't offend you or cross any lines by doing that. I just had to have a taste of you. A small taste, but it's what I'll be satisfied with for now. It is my hope that one day I'll be able to kiss you from your head all the way down to those adorable toes."

"Ahmad, I appreciate you being here for me. You're the best waiter that I know so I already trust that you'll do just as well as my house bartender/bar manager. And by the way, that kiss was wonderful. Now, how about we get to work before the others arrive. I need to begin checking in the vendors and make sure my stylist has my dresses for tonight" I said to Ahmad.

"Okay, you're the boss," Ahmad responded before he sauntered towards the bar.

Having that little moment with Ahmad really put my mind into overdrive, but I didn't have time to focus on that because at that moment the vendors began coming in, so I had to officially step into my event planner shoes.

The rest of the evening seemed to fly by. Before I knew it, I was in my luxurious office getting dressed. Two weeks of a strict diet had my body snatched in all the right places, and my glam team had really outdone themselves this year. My dress had been custom made, and it fit all of my curves just like I had hoped.

As I waited for my girls to make their grand entrances, I said a quick prayer to God and thanked him for taking my vision of being my own businesswoman and elevating it to me owning Lyric's Loft and laying the foundation to me becoming financially independent of Xavier. I knew that once the guests saw the beauty of this building and experienced the magic that it had to offer, they would be lining up to reserve Lyric's Loft for their events. With the holiday season quickly approaching, this was the easiest way to advertise and introduce Lyric's Loft to the city.

I was pulled away from my thoughts by a knock on my door.

"Come in" I called out as I stood and smoothed my dress.

"Hey Ms. Thang," drawled Christopher as he sauntered into the room looking stunning in a three piece suit.

"Hi Chris. Are you ready for me?"

"Yes Ms. Thang. The other heifers have already made their grand entrances, and honey I must admit those heifers were fierce!!"

I couldn't help but giggle as Christopher marched around my office showing me how Sheree, Morgan, and Maven had sashayed into the party.

"Well now Mr. Thang, it's time for me to make my grand entrance and announce to all of the movers and shakers of the city, along with my family and friends, that they are looking at the new owner of Lyric's Loft".

I did a little Kenya Moore Gone-With-the-Wind Fabulous twirl, which caused the train of my gorgeous gown to billow into the air like a parachute on a windy day, put my arm into Christopher's arm, and walked out onto the balcony overlooking the main floor of Lyric's Loft. I stood there for a minute enjoying the view of the crowd and the beautiful décor before I made my way to the custom dance floor.

I remember taking the microphone and thanking everyone for coming out to celebrate our birthdays. I remember everyone applauding and cheering as I called Maven, Morgan, and Sheree on to the dance floor for our customary, before the turn-up begins group photo that we do every year.

What I remember the most about that moment was the look on Xavier's face when I announced to the guests, my family, and my friends that I, in fact, was the proud owner of Lyric's Loft and the Morgan Ferber Event Planning Group. Although Xavier pretended that he was happy and excited for me by clapping and even coming on to the dance floor to hug me and plant a kiss on my forehead, I could tell by the tight grip on my arm that he was definitely pissed that I had beat him at his own game by keeping a secret from him. I also knew that in Xavier's mind he was realizing that me taking control of my own life and finances meant that he would no longer be able to hold me as a financial hostage.

As if he could read my thoughts, they were interrupted by Xavier's footsteps outside of our bedroom door and I'm brought back to the present. I brace myself because I know that what I'm about to tell Xavier will be a major turning point in both of our lives. I say a quick prayer because I don't know how Xavier is going to handle it. Even though he hasn't slept in the same bed as me since the paternity test fiasco, I still love Xavier. The question is, "Am I still IN love with Xavier?" The fact that I have just an inkling of doubt about it is the final factor in the decision that I have made.

"Hi Shaina," he says as he walks in. "About last night. Although I am happy that you've decided to reenter the work force, I still think that it was very tacky the way you waited to tell me, your husband, at the same time that you told a room full of strangers," Xavier spits at me as he begins to pace back and forth around the bedroom.

I steady my voice before addressing Xavier because I don't want him to know how much he is pissing me off right now! As many times as he has kept some scandalous, adulterous, soul-breaking lies, he gets upset that I kept a secret that was meant to give me financial freedom.

I want to tell him to have several seats but instead I say, "Well, Xavier, I understand that you weren't happy about me purchasing Lyric's Loft behind your back, and I'm okay with that. And since we're on the subject of you not agreeing with my decisions, I have one more decision that I'm sure you're not going to understand, like, or agree with, but I'm okay with that too."

"Shaina, what in the hell are you talking about? What decision could you have made now, and why are you choosing to share this one with me?" Xavier asks as he stops pacing the room long enough to come and sit on the edge of the bed.

"Xavier, you know that I've loved you for more than half of my life. You gave me the other love of my life, our beautiful daughter. You've been by my side through many tough times in my life, and at one point I could not see myself being without you in my life."

He once again stands up, this time coming to kneel in front of me. "Shaina. I don't like the sound of this. Baby, I-"

I interrupt Xavier and continue. "However, you also know that our marriage has suffered throughout the years, and I feel like I've lost myself in the process."

Xavier takes my hands into his. He stares at me long and hard and I can see tears welling up in the corner of his eyes. I can tell that his breathing is becoming more labored by the moment. "So what are you saying Shaina?"

"Xavier, I've decided that I need time to work on me and building my life without being in your shadow or being your wife. So, as of today Xavier we are officially separated. I'm leaving you and taking Lyric with me. Morgan should be sending you the paperwork tomorrow. Lyric and I will be leaving after my brunch with the girls."

With that, I ignore the incredulous look on Xavier's face and walk into the bathroom to shower and prepare for the brunch.

Chapter Thirty-Eight

Maven

"When you don't give people the right information, you give them permission to use their imagination."

Wow. As I stand under the hot water from the showerhead cascading down my body, I can't help but think back to our birthday party last night!! Now, don't get me wrong over the years we've experienced our share of amazing birthday parties from a 90s jam to casino night to a straight up Reggae throw down, but I must say that last night might have topped them all.

My night started off on a high because for the first time in years, I had a date for the party, and not just a family member or a friend of a friend, or Cash, but this year a real live, breathing, sexy, catering to my every need man who would be my side.

Houston and I had pretty much been inseparable since our first date, and although he had flown back to Atlanta a week ago, I was more than happy that he had gotten back just in time to be my date for tonight. And boy does that man know how to impress a woman. I was

195

at the salon yesterday when Cash and Karver both came waltzing into my office. Each of them was carrying a dozen yellow long-stemmed roses.

"Oh you guy are so sweet! Thanks for the roses. You can put them over there on my desk", I squealed with delight.

"Um boss lady, pump your brakes," Karver said.

Cash agreed. "Yeah boss lady. I mean, we love you and all, but you already know I don't have any money to buy you two dozens of roses. You must have forgotten how much you pay us!"

"Very funny guys. Well, if you didn't buy the roses. Who did?" I asked.

"I did," called out a deep, sexy voice, and at that very moment the door to my office eased open and there stood Houston. I stood by my desk in shock because I knew that he had flown back to Atlanta, but I didn't know that he would be coming back before the party.

"Houston. What are you doing here? I thought you were still in Atlanta?" I said walking towards him as he stopped to fist bump Karver and Cash.

"Thanks guys for helping me. I owe y'all."

"No problem," Karver said. "You're like a brother man."

"Well not to me," joked Cash. "I want my money now bruh." Houston couldn't help but laugh.

Cash and Karver then hugged me goodbye and made their way out of my office.

"Maven, when I was in Atlanta, I couldn't get my mind off of you and how you would be attending that party tomorrow night alone. When I thought about the possibility of another man holding you close to his body while the two of you danced the night away, there was no way that I could let that happen, so I canceled the rest of my plans and meetings that I had in Atlanta, hopped on the first flight that I could find, and came straight to you," Houston explained.

I couldn't believe my ears. No man had ever cancelled any plans to be with me. Usually they just cancelled their plans with me to be with someone else.

"Houston, I don't know what to say. You don't even know how much this means to me," I said as he pulled me into his warm embrace.

"Just say that you'll allow me to hold you just like this on the dance floor tomorrow night," Houston responded as he began to slowly rub my back.

I stepped out of Houston's embrace. "No problem honey, but you must have forgotten how we used to dance back in the day. You know I like to back that ass up," I said to Houston as I did an impromptu booty shaking session.

Houston laughed and came up behind me grinding his pelvis into my booty. I leaned back onto his chest and enjoyed our little spontaneous dance session.

"Well sweetie, as much as I'm enjoying you right now, I know that you need to finish up here, and I need to go out to the barbershop area so that Karver can get me right for tomorrow night."

"Yes. Please do. I'm going to be looking extra hot tomorrow so I can't have you looking all raggedy on my arm."

"Ha ha, very funny Maven. Now give daddy a kiss," Houston requested.

I chuckled, gave him a kiss, and walked back to my desk to finish going through emails and paperwork.

About ten minutes later, I was once again interrupted by a knock on my office door.

"Come on in, it's open," I called out.

I looked up from my computer to see Karver coming through the door with a big smile on his face.

"Boss Lady I'm sorry to disturb you, but I have some news that I wanted to share with you."

"Well, by the look of that smile on your face, I'm going to guess that this time it's good news."

"Yes. Well, hopefully it will lead to the news that I've been waiting on my whole life. Remember I was going to talk to the private investigator today?" Karver asked.

"What? Your birth mom? They found her? Where is she? When are you going to see her?" I questioned Karver, full of excitement.

"Slow down Maven," Karver told me.

"Sorry Karver. I just know how important finding your mom is to you."

"Yes it is, and now we finally have a lead. The private investigator just called me. He told me that he had a match that is a 90-95% chance she could be my birth mother."

"Oh wow Karver. That's amazing!"

"I know right. And guess what? They even have her name. It's Gloria."

"Gloria?" I repeated to Karver.

"Yes", he said. "Isn't that crazy? I finally know a possible name to my possible birth mother."

I saw Karver's mouth moving, but I didn't actually hear another word that came out of his mouth.

Gloria was also my mother's name, and although it was a little farfetched to think that if could be her who was Karver's birth mother, it definitely wasn't impossible. I had always heard rumors about my mom having a son before I was born, but I just thought it was project gossip.

I mean, now as I sat there looking at Karver standing in front of me I studied his features more closely. He did share many of the same features as some of the other members of my family.

"You okay Boss Lady," Karver asked me with a worried look forming on his face.

"Sorry Karver. I was just thinking how happy I am for you. When will you know something for sure?"

"The private investigator told me that he's planning to meet with me Monday morning so that I can sign some paperwork and that he'll give me more details then. Thanks for having my back and being my friend Boss Lady. I'm gonna head back out to the shop so that I can finish getting your man ready for tomorrow night."

"No problem Karver. Thanks for all you do around here, especially getting my man ready," I said with a smile.

As soon as Karver left my office, I plopped down into my chair. My mind was racing with so many thoughts but there was one that stood out. Was it possible that Karver was my brother?

I hear the shower door opening and then I feel Houston's presence behind me, which brings me back to the present and causes my body to immediately respond to him. All thoughts of Karver and his birth mother go out the window.

"Hey sweetie. I was getting lonely in the bed waiting on you so I decided to come find out if you needed any help," Houston teases as his fingers begin to make their way down my neck to cup my breasts.

I moan in pleasure as Houston's hands are soon replaced by his mouth. I feel my knees begin to buckle and a sense of relief and frustration when Karver tells me to dry off and get back in bed to wait on him.

We kiss long and hard before I stepped out of the shower, leaving him to wash off quickly.

"Baby will you put my phone on the charger? I need to get some juice before we leave for brunch at Rico's," Houston asks.

"No problem baby. Now hurry up because I have some juice of my own that I want to give to you."

"I can't wait."

I walk back to the bedroom and am getting ready to crawl back into bed when I remember that Houston asked me to put his phone on the charger. Picking up his phone from the tuxedo pants that he wore last night, I walk to put in on the charger on the nightstand when it starts to ring. I was going to ignore it, but stop in my tracks when the word "Wifey" appears on the screen.

Standing there as naked as the day I was born, I contemplate throwing the phone across the room, but I decide that I need the phone to be in good working condition when I confront Houston. Although I'm absolutely on fire inside, I try my best to contain my anger until I can get an explanation from him.

As if he can read my thoughts, Houston comes out of the bathroom at that very moment.

I didn't give him a chance to say anything.

"Houston. What the hell is this?" I yell out while holding his phone in my hand so that he can see the missed call from "Wifey".

"Maven baby, it's not what you think. I can explain."

Chapter Thirty-Nine

Sheree

"When you're looking for more, more will always be willing and waiting. Be content with what you have."

To say I'm one tired bitch is an understatement. My neck. My back. My feet. My ass. Everything, and I do mean everything, on my body is sore. Most of that is due to my all night freak session with Marcus.

Yeah, I know some people will be thinking, "How can she talk about Tyrell cheating when was sexing her boy toy?"

Well, I have several things to say in response to that. First of all, Tyrell started this. I was faithful to him for too damn long while he was out there chasing ass. I didn't cheat on him for the first time until he went to jail. Hell, why should I punish myself for his dumb ass mistakes?

Second of all, when it comes to Marcus, this was our first time actually having sexual intercourse. Usually we would just get together and hug and kiss, and of course, he always wanted to taste my Candy, which I never have a problem with because he does such a good job.

Last of all, Tyrell and I have been broken up for over a month now, and Marcus has been there for me the entire time, and not just sexually. He was right there in the hospital when I had my severe anxiety attack. Marcus didn't leave my side until I made him go home. So I think that he earned the right to snuggle with this big chocolate ass of mine for at least one night.

Besides, as tipsy as I was last night, there was no way that I was coming home alone. Somebody was going to be my victim, so why not make it somebody that had already had a sample of what I had to offer? Not someone like Tyrell who knew what I had to offer, but still wanted to go online to see if he could find something better.

Speaking of Tyrell, I couldn't believe that he had the nerves to show his ass up at the party last night. The girls and I were upstairs in Shaina's office/dressing room getting ready to make our customary wardrobe change when Christopher's messy ass came sashaying through the door.

"Um. Ms. Thang Sheree," he called out. "I don't know if you are aware of this but your most recent boyfriend, Mr. Tyrell, just walked in. I didn't know if y'all were back together again or not, so I thought I would give you the heads-up."

For one moment I thought about telling security to kick his ass all the way from the entrance back to his car, but then I decided that I wasn't going to let Tyrell's ass ruin our night. "No. It's fine Christopher. Tell security to let him stay. I want him to see all that he's been missing out on since I put him and his shit out of my house. I'm here to enjoy my birthday with my girls, and I definitely won't let my tired ass trifling ex stop me from doing just that."

And I didn't. After my wardrobe change, I strutted my sexy ass downstairs and walked right up to Tyrell. He took a step back. I don't know if he was scared that I was gonna slap the shit out of him or if he was just trying to get a closer look at my ASSets that were on full blast.

"Thanks for coming," I said to Tyrell. "I hope that you enjoy yourself as much as I'm going to enjoy myself." I turned around to walk away from him. Tyrell grabbed my arm, and I gave him a look that I'm sure burned through his shirt.

"Look, Sheree. Just give me a minute please," he requested. "Just know that you were the best thing that has happened in my life for a long time. I know that I've hurt you bad and there's nothing that I can say right now to make up for that. Know that I'll always have mad love for you and what you did for me over the years and loving me when I didn't deserve it. I'm truly sorry."

It seemed as if time stood still for a moment as I listened to Tyrell's heartfelt words. It had been a long time since he'd said anything so sweet and sincere to me. I felt tears begin to well in my eyes as I became angry that he would choose now to confess his love for me, and I also felt sad because I still loved him. But as much as his words touched my heart, my mind would not let me forget what he had done. Thoughts of him screwing another woman in my bed and images of me laying in that hospital bed not knowing if I was having a heart attack or not quickly replaced any sappy ass loving feelings that I was having for him.

I blinked the tears away before responding to Tyrell. "Yes. You are sorry Tyrell. A sorry ass excuse for a man." And with that I walked away from him forever this time, making sure to jiggle my plump ass a little harder because I knew his eyes would stay on me until I was out of sight.

The rest of the night went by in a blur. I danced. I ate. I drank and drank some more. Snuck in a few grinding sessions with Marcus and a few others on the dance floor. Damn near tripped over the train of my dress. Ate some more. Drank some more, and had a damn good time. I must say that Shaina's little sneaky ass really outdid herself this time.

That party last night was over the top and worth waking up with a sore body. Speaking of bodies, I begin to feel the body stirring beside me, and I was reminded that I was waking up with much more than a sore body this morning. For the first time since we met, I had finally allowed Marcus to spend an entire night next to me, and I am so glad that I had. He was a magnificent lover. Gentle, but a little rough. Just like I like it. Plus he had stamina. We had literally screwed each other to sleep, and then started all over again.

By the third time Marcus woke me up, I was so tired that all I could do was lay there and let him have his way with my body. He rode me for what seemed like an hour until he released himself and fell asleep on my chest.

"Hey my chocolate cake. How are you this morning?" Marcus asks me sleepily.

I look down and see his hardness sticking straight up underneath the sheet.

"Well, I see someone is up and ready this morning," I say to him.

"I told you babe, he stays ready. Especially for a taste of your sweet Candy."

"That's good to know, and I'm actually in the mood to do some tasting of my own this morning.

I begin to stoke Marcus's hard shaft, licking my lips in anticipation when all of a sudden my doorbell rings.

"What the hell? Who in their right damn mind would have the nerve to show up at my house at 7:00 a.m.? On a Sunday morning? Without calling or texting me first?

At first I think it could be Tyrell, but I know how scared he is that I will call the police. The girls all have keys to my house, so I know it wasn't one of them. And my family, well they already know better than to show up unannounced.

I kiss the tip of Marcus's manhood. "Keep him hard and ready for Mama. I'll be right back."

Hurrying to find something to throw on, I rush downstairs to continuous knocks on the door and rings from the doorbell.

"I'm coming!" I yell as I snatch the front door open to find my sister, Zoe, standing at my front door.

"Zoe? What are you doing here? Why didn't you call me to tell me you were coming? How'd you get here? Well, come on in. It's a little chilly out here," I say as I wave her in.

I step back into the foyer and wait on Zoe to come in. I notice that she has a few pieces of luggage which would suggest that she was planning on staying for a while. I'll address that later. For now, I need to find out what has brought her here.

"Zoe. What's up?"

"How could you? I thought that you loved me Sheree. How could you do this to me?" she says as she starts to cry.

"Hold on Zoe. What in the hell are you talking about?" I ask, confused as to what I could have done to her.

"Cut the dumb shit Sheree! You know exactly what I'm talking about!, Zoe shouts at me.

I plead with her, "Zoe. Please tell me what's going on?"

"You already know. You've known my entire life. You and mom. Yet the two of you didn't think I would ever find out."

Oh no. I can't believe this shit is happening. Not now. My mind is racing, but I hear Zoe loud and clear when she softens her voice and says to me, "Why didn't you tell me Sheree? Why didn't you tell me that you're not my sister? You're my mother."

Chapter Forty

Morgan

"You can always turn a purposeful mess into an accidental success."

The alarm on my phone is really annoying to me this morning. Usually I'm a morning person, but I'm just not feeling like my normal myself today.

I know it isn't from last night because honestly I don't remember drinking any alcoholic beverages the entire night. I tried to take a sip of my normal Vodka and cranberry juice, but just a whiff of it made me sick to my stomach, so for the rest of the night, I drank ginger ale. I attributed my queasy stomach to all of the stress that I have been experiencing lately in both my professional and personal lives.

First of all, there was a major setback at my office. A few weeks ago, MariCruz came into my office on a Monday morning looking like she had been in a fight with Ronda Rousey. When I asked her what was wrong, she just said that she couldn't talk about it.

I didn't want to pry, so I didn't push her for answers. She then informed me that she would need to take a few weeks off and from the black eye, the busted lip, and the numerous cuts and scratches on her neck and face. I knew that taking a few weeks off was the best thing for her to do. I told MariCruz that I hoped she would be okay and not to hesitate to call me if she needed anything.

I mean MariCruz had been with me for more than three years, so it was definitely hard for me to see her like that. But I know that she's always been a very private person which means I wouldn't know what happened to her until, or better yet, if and when she was ready to confide in me.

That had been more than a month ago, and MariCruz said that she still wasn't ready to come back to work. I informed her that she should take her time, but I had to hire someone else in the meantime. Thankfully the temp service sent over a wonderful young man who happened to be the son of one of my colleagues at another firm in the city.

His name was Dominic Miguel, and he was simply amazing. Whether MariCruz returned or not, I had already offered him a full-time position, and of course he had accepted.

If only things were going that smoothly with my dealings with Xavier. He has been calling me and dropping by my office unannounced almost daily for the past six weeks. No matter how many times I ignore his calls or text messages or kick him out of my office, he still keeps trying to see me.

For what? What did he think would or could happen with us? What we did had been one night of passion under the influence of alcohol. He can't possibly think that there could be a repeat of that night? Well, it doesn't matter what Xavier wants. I don't want anything from him, and I try my best to not have to be in the same room with him alone.

And I almost succeeded until last night of course. I guess a little part of me was holding out hope that, considering the state of his and Shaina's marriage, Xavier wouldn't even show up, and if his arrogant behind did decide to show up he would only speak to me and then keep it moving. What was I thinking? Xavier had always had a sense of entitlement and had been a cocky son-of-a-bitch ever since I met him, so I don't know what made me think that last night would be any different.

The night was going wonderfully. I was having a great time despite my upset stomach. I was even able to shake my thang on the dance floor. I guess I was shaking a little too much because all of a sudden I felt everything that I had eaten in the past hour begin to bubble up in my stomach. I rushed off the dance floor and down the hall to find the nearest ladies' room.

I barely made it into a stall before I was emptying the contents of my belly into the toilet. After about a minute of spasms and vomiting, I started to feel a little better. I walked to the sink to rinse my mouth and wipe the sweat from my face. I was thankful that the restroom attendant had a basket of toiletries including mouthwash and peppermint, which I needed at that time.

After checking to make sure that I didn't look like I had just finished vomiting, I walked out of the restroom and ran straight into a hard chest. I didn't have to look up to know that it was Xavier. I knew his scent. It had been engraved in my mind ever since our night of passion.

"Morgan. Are you okay? I saw you run off the dance floor, and I wanted to check on you," Xavier said as I took a few steps back to get away from him.

"I'm fine Xavier. Just think I had too much to drink," I lied, hoping that he would leave me alone.

"Now Morgan. Remember what happened the last time that you had a little too much to drink."

"You are such an arrogant ass Xavier! For your information, you need to stay out of my business and tend to your own business with your wife while you still have one!"

"I apologize Morgan. I'm really concerned that you're acting like what happened between us didn't happen," Xavier said as he moved towards me.

I looked at Xavier straight in his green eyes and spat out, "As far as I'm concerned, it didn't happen." I spun on my heels and walked, half-ran back to the main party room with Xavier following close behind. Luckily, he was interrupted by one of his fraternity brothers, which gave me time to get the hell away from him.

The rest of the night was pretty uneventful. I was able to enjoy my night with my family and friends without being approached by Xavier again, although I could feel his eyes on me throughout the night.

"Auntie M?" Niecey calls from outside my bedroom door, taking me out of my thoughts.

"It's open Niecey. Come on in."

"Good morning Auntie. I just wanted to know if it's okay if Mahogany came to brunch with us today."

"That's fine Niecey. Call her and tell her to be ready by 11:00."

"Auntie? Did you forget that Mahogany spent the night here last night?"

"Yes. I did," I admit to Niecey. "Must have been too much fun from last night."

"I guess," Niecey says giving me the side eye.

I can't help but smile as I think about how grateful I am to have Niecey in my life. In fact, as of now, I am her legal guardian on paper although Tish has calmed down a whole lot and wants Niecey back at home with her.

When Niecey found out, she told both of us that she didn't want to leave my home. I could tell that Tish was really hurt, but she stayed true to her tough ass persona and pretended like that was okay with her. She had even agreed to sign over parental guardianship to me, and I couldn't have been more thrilled.

I really enjoy having Niecey in my home. We have so much fun together. Most nights we cook dinner or order take-out and sit around eating and watching movies. Now we are in the process of preparing Niecey to take her ACT and SATs. She's been studying extremely hard, and I'm still thankful that I'm able to provide her with a loving, nurturing environment. Since I have just about given up on being able to conceive and have a child of my own, I will just try to be the best auntie and guardian to Niecey that I can be.

Oh no. That nauseous sensation that has become all too familiar over the past few weeks begins to move around in my stomach again. I quickly jump out of bed and made a beeline to my bathroom, almost knocking Niecey down as she is coming in my room at the same time.

I make it to the bathroom just in time, falling to my knees, hugging the toilet as if it was my best friend, and releasing the contents of my stomach. As soon as I think it's was over, I'm hit with more waves of nausea, which causes me to heave and cry. My body trembles in pain as I wait for the dizziness and queasiness to be gone.

I don't know how long I sit on the cold bathroom floor hugging the toilet. I hear Niecey calling out to me, "Auntie. Are you okay? You need me to bring you anything?"

I get up from the floor, wash my face with cold water, make my way to my bed, and crawl in it to lay down.

Niecey comes to me with a glass of ginger ale.

"Here Auntie. This should make you feel better."

"Thanks Niecey. I don't know what's been going on with my belly lately."

"Well Auntie," Niecey says as she walks out my bedroom door. "If I had seen you with a boyfriend, I would say that you could be pregnant. This is how Tish was when she was pregnant with Jay and Kadina."

I damn near drop the glass of ginger ale on the carpet.

Pregnant? There's no way that I can be pregnant. I have been told since I was twelve years old that I only have a small chance of ever conceiving a child.

Pregnant? I can't stop saying that word. I jump up from the bed to grab my phone from my purse. I hurriedly scroll through until I find what I was looking for.

My calendar. I always keep up with my monthly cycle in my calendar. My heart literally stops when I realize that the last time I had a period was eight weeks ago, right before that night of passion that I had shared with Xavier.

This can not be happening to me. I have prayed to God every night for as long as I can remember that He allow me to one day be able to conceive and give birth to my own child. Although I know that God answered prayers, I also know that being molested almost completely destroyed my chances to ever get pregnant on my own.

Even as I try to convince myself otherwise, I have been around too many pregnant women to ignore the signs. My tender swollen breasts that I attributed to hormones or being horny. The nausea and vomiting, which I told myself was just stress. The increased urination, which I just knew came from increasing my water intake. And lastly the fatigue, which I attributed to the long nights at the office.

Still trying to convince myself that all of these could just be signs of something else, I remember that Sheree had left a pregnancy test here just two months ago when she was thinking that she was pregnant. I go into my bathroom and rummage through the drawers until I find it. I quickly read the directions, pee on the stick, and sit it on the top of the toilet to wait for the results.

For 10 minutes I pace the floor in my bedroom and finally decided that I can't wait any longer. That walk to the bathroom seems to be the longest walk of my life because I know the results can and will change me forever.

As I get close to the pregnancy test, there is no turning back. I pick it up and fell the bottom drop from my stomach. Two lines.

I can't ignore it any longer. I'm pregnant. Based on the fact that I haven't been with any other men in more than eight months ago, I'm pregnant by Xavier. One of my best friend's husband.

Discussion Questions for Love, Lies, & Loyalty

1. What is your overall impression of this book?

2. Who was your favorite character?

3. Which character was most like you? Least like you?

4. Which character represents someone in your family? Your circle of friends?

5. Thinking about Sheree, have you ever had a "Tyrell" in your life? What did he or she finally do to make you leave?

6. Was Shaina wrong to keep such important news from Xavier?

7. Were you surprised at the way Morgan's story played out in the book?

8. Are there times when you have wanted to "divorce" your family?

9. How should Maven handle the situation with her old flame?

10. Which girl's story do you think should come next, or do you think the next book should include all of them again?

Connect with the Author

Website: www.authorsheliasewell.com

Facebook: Author Shelia Sewell

Instagram: ImjustShelia

Twitter: ImjustShelia

Made in the USA
Columbia, SC
13 June 2021

39319061R10128